Arranged MATING

OTHERWORLDERS SERIES

CHRIS ROGERS

Arranged Mating

Chris Rogers

Arranged MATING

OTHERWORLDERS SERIES

CHRIS ROGERS

CHAPTER 1

Isla could recite her grandfather's speech by heart. It had been drilled into her since he took her in when she was twelve.

"With the breakouts occurring in the Underground, which happens to hold some of the most treacherous Otherworlders, we are facing entirely new dangers. New threats that we must prepare for. Threats we have never seen before."

Isla, like many from the five species of Otherworlders, lived hidden among the human race. Demons, Vampires, Magicae, Werewolves, and Fae who did not want to live among the humans, resided in the parallel Underground. Portals created by the Counsel Witch and Warlock connected the worlds. These portals were the only gateways between the two worlds for most species. Except for the few chosen to protect The Realm.

"The rising conflict among Otherworlders is a growing concern." Isla rolled her eyes. It was too early in the morning to be lectured. "We need to strengthen our alliances and prepare for what is coming. We are sworn to protect the secrets of the Realm, to maintain balance in our world. That is why at the next wolf moon you will be mated."

Choking on her sip of coffee Isla cleared her throat, putting down her cup as she stared at her grandfather. *We are sworn to protect the Realm to maintain balance in our world. Honor. Strength. Protection. It's our duty to protect the Realm's secret from humans and those who seek to destroy it.* That's what he was supposed to say. That is what he had said for the last thirteen years.

For as long as she could remember, the Underground had been a threat. Governed by the Counsel— which was driven by power and status and run by the most powerful clans of species who feed off of others—it jailed some of the oldest and most dangerous Otherworlders who had turned Crazed during their long imprisonment and who tended to escape. Diseased, with no sense of humanity left, once escaped they would go on a rampage, as killing was the heartbeat of their existence. The Counsel of Otherworlders—made up of five elders, one representative from each of the species—believed they could rehabilitate the Crazed, and cure their disease. But two centuries later, they were no closer to a cure than when they started.

And then there was the Realm.

For some time, The Realm had encompassed all of the Underground. But then the peace was shattered by the war of the Gods. The Moon Goddess hid The Realm from Otherworlders in an attempt to protect the innocent. She refused to bow to any of the Gods or the Ancients by giving up The Realm. As punishment, she was banished from the Underground to the mortal world and stripped of her ability to walk among Otherworlders. The banishment also separated her from the Realm, never allowing her to return.

For years, Otherworlders searched for The Realm only to come up empty-handed. After centuries, the tale of The Realm became more myth than reality: a story about a place of peace run by the old and wise Fairy Rattenru. A place that Otherworlders only heard about but have never seen.

But none of that explained her Alpha's sudden announcement.

"I'm sorry Grandfather...what?"

"You are my oldest kin. My *only* kin. When I am gone you will lead this pack with a strong mate. I have been training you to be a leader. A warrior. You have the respect of this pack. They will follow you and your mate, who will be their Alpha and lead as I have. But only as long as you have a strong mate who can lead. Our pack has protected the

Realm for centuries. It is time we strengthen our alliances to continue our duty." Isla knew what her grandfather was thinking: if only she were a male. His grandson would be able to lead without a mate.

Most girls grew up playing with dolls, going on dates and dances, and exploring the free world. Not Isla. As her father never had a son, her Grandfather had accepted Isla as the eldest and had been preparing her to be the future leader of the pack since she was a young sparkling-eyed child. She was always training, and always being tested—and he had yet to invent a test she couldn't pass. In fact, she always exceeded his expectations, she made sure of it. In all of his years, he had never seen anyone quite like her. And he didn't even know the secret she'd kept hidden from him. She had hoped one day he would accept her as a leader of the pack without a mate, as would any male heir. But deep down she had always known it was an empty hope.

"Grandfather, you have got to be kidding me. A mate? I don't need a mate to lead! You've trained me well. So I'm saying no." That wasn't entirely true. Isla would eventually need a mate who was a Werewolf, who could shift and run with the pack to lead them. As a female wolf, that was the one thing she could not do –– shift. Male werewolves had the ability to shift to wolf form. Powerful, skilled werewolves could shift into their hybrid form. But males needed females with were-blood to breed the next pureblooded generation. Though valued mostly for their childbearing qualities, many females also possessed a skill or a heightened ability. When werewolves mated, their strengths and abilities combined, making their offspring even more deadly. Isla's gift was her heightened ability as a skilled fighter.

CHAPTER 2

Isla watched her grandfather's face harden into his alpha-mask.

"You are an exceptional warrior. When I look at you, I see your mother. But you have the heart and spirit of your father. However, it is time we formed an alliance with another pack to strengthen our numbers. I have given this much thought and it is our best—and really only—option."

Was he serious? "Given *this* much thought? Without even talking to me?" Her temper surfaced. How could he? "You are talking about *my* life. You expect me to just fall in love with someone *you* choose?" Isla stared at her grandfather, barely believing she was even having this conversation with him. No longer hungry, she pushed her still-full breakfast plate aside.

Winston raised his brows. "Isla, love is an emotion. People like us do not have the luxury of loving. People like us only have time for honor and duty. Love is for fools."

No longer able to sit at the kitchen table, Isla stood and started pacing. "I should have a say in who my mate is going to be. After all, I will be stuck with this person for the rest of my life. Till death do us part." She had no doubt her Grandfather would see to it that she was mated. It was obvious he did not care if she ever formed a true bond with her mate. A bond between mates was sacred. To find your true mate, to be spiritually connected, was an experience blessed by the Moon Goddess herself. A blessed mating meant a long life. Werewolves were not immortal, but with a true mating they could live for hundreds of years unless they were killed forcefully. Wouldn't it be better for the pack if she could find that for herself?

Winston shook his head in disappointment at Isla's immaturity. His peppered grey hair fell over his face, temporarily hiding his frustration. "You are my granddaughter and the next pack leader. I am the Alpha, and you will obey. Your mate must have my approval as he will lead the pack with you. You are a Bane, start acting like one."

His words hit her like a bucket of ice water. Isla had not thought of taking a mate. That was the last thing she wanted. She had no intention of ever being dependent on any other man, or anyone else. She had worked her whole life to please her Alpha. To earn his respect. To be the best. And more importantly, to be accepted by him. It was unfair that after the years and years of blood, sweat, and tears she'd put in, this was the treatment she was receiving. Part of his reaction was likely due to the fact that after her parents and younger sister died the night of the attack, Winston hardened entirely. He had lost his son, and with him had lost any hope of having a male heir he could groom to be the next Alpha. Still, he wasn't the only one who had experienced that loss.

A coldness settled in Isla, calming the fury that she felt. No matter what she wanted, he was her Alpha above everything else. Narrowing her eyes, she asked, "Who is it?"

Winston looked pleased to see Isla coming to her senses. "Axel Griffith from the Shadow Pack."

Isla was speechless. Axel Griffith? Seriously? Surely, he lost his mind to want her to marry a Griffith, let alone Axel.

"He will make a good alliance. Their pack is diverse, strong in numbers, and has excellent resources."

Money. He forgot to say that they have lots of money.

Negotiations have already begun. This is what is best for the pack. Best for protecting the Realm. Winston's thoughts sent a sharp tone into Isla's head. Taking a slow, deep breath, she got up from the table, close-lipped to avoid saying anything she would regret. Winston was her

Alpha first and Grandfather second.

But seriously, Axel? Axel was egotistical and knew nothing of commitment except to himself. A known ladies' man. Isla had never met him, but he was the famous Axel, the Werewolf bachelor everyone wanted to land... Except for Isla, of course. Of all of the warriors from all the packs Winston could have chosen, he wanted Axel to become her mate? Was he even a warrior? Since he had had such a privileged life, she doubted he even knew how to fight or kill a Crazed.

Her silence brought a tight smile to Winston's face. "I knew I could count on you to see it my way." For the first time, Isla saw him as the old, hardened man that he had become years ago. His dark eyes locked in on her. They held no love, only dominance. The pack respected him as the Alpha, a wise but ruthless leader, always providing for the pack, no matter the cost. Now she realized that to him she was no different than any other female in the pack. Family or not, he controlled her future.

Taking a slow, deep breath, she pushed down the emotions that were building up, submitting to him. "No Grandfather, I don't see it your way, but I have no other choice."

The smile quickly vanished from Winston's face as his lips settled into a disappointed line. His voice flattened, "Isla I have always been clear that you would have an arranged mating that I would make the call on."

Isla did not recognize the grandfather she had known all her life. Even though he was her Alpha, she had always considered him her family. But right now, she did not care. "What you made clear is that you do not love me. If you did, you would have asked me what I want."

Winston stared are her. The silence stretched out between them, making Isla feel uncomfortable where she stood. There was no emotion on his face. No vein of anger popped out on his forehead. Just silence.

When Winston stood, the sliding of his chair broke the silence. His eyes stayed on Isla as he towered over her. Lowering her head she submitted to her Alpha. She could not fight the dominance he had over her. "An Alpha does what is best for the pack, not what is wanted. Not what one person wants. What the pack needs. If you go against me on the arranged mating you will be challenging your Alpha. Do. I. Make. Myself. Clear?"

"Crystal."

Isla walked out of the room without saying another word. She didn't know what else to do but leave. The way he spoke, the arrangement was a done deal.

CHAPTER 3

Isla could not get away fast enough. She ran across the open field and headed towards the tree line. The morning sun felt good on her skin, providing warmth when all she felt inside was emptiness and coldness. Finding the training room, she grabbed the metal whip wrapped around her wrist. To most, it looked like a fancy bracelet, but they would be foolishly mistaken. As she unsheathed her whip, it lengthened. Holding it firmly in her hand, Isla began destroying targets that were left from her last training practice. Shrapnel ricocheted in all directions. She channeled all of her anger into destroying every object she could get her hands on. When the last target was torn to pieces, Isla stood motionless in the midst of the chaos. Her breathing was heavy and sweat ran down her face as she gripped the whip in her hand, wishing there were more targets or even a Crazed to kill.

The whip had been a gift from her mother on her tenth birthday. It was made by fairies with special magic and contained a binding spell that linked it to Isla. Her mother had taught her specific weaponry skills that included how to control the whip and use it as an extension of herself. Isla's gift as a skilled fighter only made her wielding of the whip more advanced, beyond what her mother could have imagined. Since the day the attack on their pack took the lives of her parents, Isla's secret had been buried along with her mother. Now, her mother's voice echoed in her head: *Trust no one with who you are. Not your father. And especially not our Alpha.*

"Bad day?" Connor stood back when he saw Isla was on a rampage.

"Looks to me like you are one pissed-off princess."

Isla hated it when Connor referred to her as a princess. She was anything but a dainty helpless female who needed rescuing. She wiped away the hot tears that had streamed down her face during her episode, deciding to control her emotions in order to not appear as weak in front of anyone. "It's nothing." The last thing she wanted to do was talk about her arranged mating. Let alone talk about Axel Griffith.

Connor walked over to the side of the room and picked up a piece of debris. "I wouldn't call opening up a can of whoop-ass on targets nothing…" Tossing the debris in the trash he watched Isla out of the corner of his eye. He could tell she was upset and kept a safe distance. As her best friend, he knew when to be cautious around her. She was not the average female who wanted to be held and consoled when she was upset. Oh no, she was a fighter. "Just another day of hard training then?"

Isla started to pick up the mess she created and then stopped, feeling engrossed in her thoughts. "Yeah, something like that."

Isla and Connor had grown up together, though he was a few years older than Isla. She had always been a strong girl growing up. But the death of her parents had changed her entirely, causing the loss of her carefree innocence. Then again, who wouldn't be affected by a massacre?

"So, are you going to tell me what's bothering you?" Connor watched Isla as she continued to pick up debris while keeping her back to him. *Maybe she is PMSing?*

Isla wanted to roll her eyes as she heard Connor's thoughts, an ability she kept to herself. Male Werewolves could mind-link to communicate. But Isla could hear thoughts from any person nearby. As she wasn't able to talk about her gift, she had to learn how to control it herself.

Sighing, Isla glanced back at Connor. She knew he meant well. Even though he was a born warrior, his dark brown hair, tanned skin, and muscular body had a gentleness to them. At least he would have the freedom to choose his mate. She hoped he wouldn't waste the opportunity on someone who wasn't his true mate. The thought made her jealous.

There was nothing for them to talk about. The Alpha...their Alpha, was arranging for her to be mated. And that was...that. "Nothing to talk about," she said matter-of-factly. What was the point of crying about something she could not change? Isla had known this day would come. She just did not think it would be so soon. She had thought maybe she would find someone and he would be able to prove himself to her grandfather. Then again, in what world could she ever think she would live happily ever after? Those thoughts are for girls who did not have Alpha blood running through them. For those who were not destined to be the next Keeper of the Realm.

Connor threw a small piece of wood at Isla. "Hey!" Looking up, she focused on Connor.

"What do you think you're doing?"

"This is the first time you looked at me since I got here. What is going on? What is so bad that it is making you act like this? Whatever it is, it can't really be that bad."

Sighing, she shook her head. "You're right. Can't be *that* bad to find out your mating has been arranged. No big deal."

"Oh, shit." Connor didn't know what to say. This was big news. How did he not know this was happening? Had he missed an announcement?

"Yeah. Oh, *shit* is right." Isla sat down against the wall. She was exhausted. Physically and emotionally spent. Pulling her knees up, she rested her head to hide her eyes from Connor.

Quietly, Connor sat down beside her, lost in his own thoughts. "So who's the lucky wolf?" When Isla didn't respond, he started listing the names of the go-to soldiers in the pack.

Anger boiled in Isla as she listened to his amused guesses. "Stop! Just stop. He's not in our pack." Out of frustration, Isla jumped up to look down at him. He knew better than to keep teasing her with this newfound information. This was no joke to her, and it was clear she was not ready for joking. His amused smile faded as he looked up at her. Her eyes were filled with emotions, none of which were happiness.

But she couldn't be serious. *Not in the pack?* This was beyond big. Connor couldn't think of the last time a pack leader was mated to someone outside the pack. Then again, he couldn't remember the last time a female Werewolf was the oldest in the Bane bloodline. "That doesn't make sense. Are you sure? Someone outside the pack wouldn't know our traditions. They wouldn't know the first thing about protecting The Realm."

Isla said nothing and looked down at the ground to avoid his curious brown eyes.

"Who could Winston possibly want you to have as your mate?"

Isla didn't know what angered her more. The way Connor said it, or the fact that she was being treated like property? Either way, she was done with the conversation. "Not your concern." Before Connor could say another word, Isla got up and left.

CHAPTER 4

Pre-arranged mating was not uncommon among Otherworlders, especially for those of high rank or position. Title was *everything*. Title represented power. Isla recognized this and understood her duty but that didn't mean she wanted it. Since her parent's death, she had never questioned her grandfather, her Alpha. She had always worked hard to outperform others in the pack, even though she was a female and would never have the ability to transform into a Werewolf. Male Werewolves were stronger than her, but she made sure she could hold her own when competing against them. When it came to weaponry, she had a gift for wielding her whip––a skill that was well respected in her pack. She was a warrior.

Now her Alpha was focused on her being properly mated to Axel. So that became her purpose as well. Isla didn't know the first thing about being proper, nor did she care to. Being mated had not been at the top of her priority list, until recently anyway. Over the last several days her training had shifted to teaching her how to be much more presentable. She was constantly corrected on what she said and how she said it. What she looked like. How she walked. Any moment she could escape from being around her Alpha, she ran off into the woods. Sometimes she just needed peace and quiet, and a place to be herself. However, even in those moments of peace, her mind was flooded with Winston's constant berating.

You can do this better.

You always need to be presentable. You need to ensure he desires you.

This mating is only final at the next wolf moon. You need to work extra hard to be accepted. Wanted.

Isla, our pack's future is dependent on your mating. Don't you want what is best for the pack?

CHAPTER 5

The drive to the Griffith estate felt like it took an eternity. Winston was quiet as Isla stared out the window, watching the thick forest pass by. She had never been to the Griffiths' territory before, which made her wonder what lay hidden between these new trees.

Don't. Mess. This. Up. His expectations took their toll on Isla, but she kept it hidden relatively well. Winston had made it clear that what she felt did not matter, so she might as well mask what she felt--even though her chest was tight with mixed emotions of anxiety and fear. She could not help but wonder what might happen if she failed.

Isla had no desire to try to form relations with the Shadow Pack. What was the point? Still, the only way out of the arrangement would be if her Alpha decided to call it off. Would Winston change his mind? Not unless hell froze over. Going back on a decision like this would invoke war between the packs...that is, unless the Shadow Pack's Alpha declined the mating. But that would never happen either.

This would be the first of many gatherings between now and the next wolf moon which Isla would be expected to attend. Most young girls dreamed about being mated and having kids, but not Isla. No, she had focused on her duties and the responsibility of protecting The Realm. But now Winston's mind was made up and there was nothing more to be done.

Isla did not know how it made her feel, not having a choice in the pre-arranged mating. Sure, she had been mad when Winston first told her but there really wasn't much she could do--she knew she had a responsibility to serve her pack.

But now, the drive to the gathering brought on a new set of feelings that she could not place. She knew it was the way things had to be. But now that it was happening––really happening––the thought of being forced to have Axel as a mate made her shudder. He was not known for being a warrior. Far from it. And she would have to lead alongside him. Was this what fear felt like?

Isla's thoughts of Axel quickly dissipated as they pulled up to the Griffith estate. The thick forest cleared into a large, open, well-manicured property. Exotic cars lined the long driveway, and guests who were dressed in their gala attire and expensive jewelry gracefully walked into the estate home. "I thought you said this would be a small affair," Isla mumbled, knowing full well that her alpha had no control over the guest list. The Griffiths were, unsurprisingly, known for their lavish parties and gatherings.

Every window in the massive mansion was lit up and glowing brightly. The closer they drove up to the mansion the harder she found it to breathe. Doubts started to take over her mind. She couldn't do this. Could she? Bile rose in her throat as the desire to escape built up inside her, but she took a slow deep breath and pushed her emotions back down. Winston would be displeased if she got sick, as it would show she had no control over her emotions.

Stepping out of the car slowly, Isla felt small standing in front of such an extravagant home. After taking another deep breath, she followed her grandfather who entered the estate and joined the crowd that made its way to the ballroom. Warriors with heavy arms under their expensive black jackets lined the entryway, their eyes focusing on her as she walked past. Did they know who she was? With her head held high, she stayed focused on getting to the ballroom without incident. When she finally stepped into the massive, open room, with floor-to-ceiling windows stretched to the heights of arched ceilings, she was in awe. Lights sparkled as they danced through the crystal chandeliers. The walls were decorated with paintings and mirrors. Music and chatter danced through the air. And behind the lavishness, through the windows, Isla could see the moon. The sight brought her comfort, assuring her that the Moon Goddess would be watching tonight.

Before long, Winston was surrounded by a group of people, all of whom greeted him and talked about how long it had been since they'd last seen each other. Before Isla could break away, a loud booming voice filled the space. "Winston Bane, my dear old friend."

Game time.

Isla could not help but tap into Garrett's thoughts: *She's prettier than he led on. We will see if she can make it in our world, if she can adjust and be fit to mate my son.*

CHAPTER 6

"Mr. Griffith…"

"Please call me Garrett, we are practically family." Practically being the key word, Isla thought as she forced a sweet smile. Even though she knew Garrett was skeptical about her, she decided to put on her best game face. He stood tall as he towered over her. His stone-grey eyes swept over her, assessing her. The average female would have been intimidated by his cold wandering eyes, let alone by his presence—except Isla remained calm and met his stare. She was not someone who let others intimidate her and wasn't afraid to show it.

Lilly, Garrett's wife, linked her arm with Isla and said, "Come Isla, let's grab a drink while these men take their time catching up." As they walked away, Isla had no doubt that the Alphas had gone straight to talking about business––the arranged mating, to be specific. Winston never wasted any time, or an opportunity for that matter.

"Isla, how did you take the news when dear old Winston told you about Axel?" Lilly was sweet, soft-spoken, and graceful. No apparent hidden agenda. Lilly's blond hair laid perfectly around her face, not a strand out of place. Her soft porcelain skin was flawless. Her presence made Isla self––conscious of how she stood next to her––part of her feeling out of place. Isla searched Lilly's mind, genuinely interested in her thoughts, or at least what she had to say about the arranged mating.

It was a relief to find herself around someone who was not thinking one thing and saying another. There was plenty of noise in the air with people looking at her and wondering, *Is that her?* Silently judging her, even though they didn't know her. Closing off her mind, she took a drink from a waiter and just held it. The thought of drinking alcohol right now churned her stomach, as her nerves from the car ride still hadn't settled. "Lilly, to be honest, I am not sure what to think or expect. The news was a complete surprise. I don't know Axel, I've never met him, so I'm trying to keep an open mind about it all." Isla had heard a lot about him. His parties. His nightlife. And how he always had female company...And sometimes more than one. She wondered how often it occurred. Would he expect that of her? Would he continue having others keep him company after they were mated? Her head spun.

As Lilly scanned the crowd, she interrupted her internal turmoil, saying, "Well he's around here somewhere, I'm sure. You want to know something? Garrett and I were matched by our parents ages ago. I remember when my father told me he had arranged for me to be mated, I was absolutely furious. I knew Garrett and I personally did not care for him." She smiled at the memory. *I did more than not care for him. I despised him.*

Lilly opening up was like a breath of fresh air. However, even though she felt she could trust her, Isla kept her guard up. Something felt off to her about the whole situation, but she couldn't place her finger on it. Lilly told stories about how Garrett had been unkind to her in school and how much she had disliked him. When she found out her father was arranging for her to mate Garrett, she was beside herself. "But I trusted my daddy. It took some time to form a relationship, as Garrett was very popular with the ladies. He did not make it easy." Like father, like son. "But once we had established our relationship, everything changed. It is indescribable what it is like to be bonded to your mate. Over time, you become one. Forming a true mating is...well words cannot describe the feeling." Lilly's look across the room to Garrett was heartwarming. Almost on cue, Garrett caught Lilly's eyes and acknowledged her. Unspoken words were exchanged between them. Perhaps there would be a chance for happiness for Isla and Axel after all. She did hope for it, but she wasn't holding her breath.

Isla wondered how much Lilly really knew of Axel's reputation and involvement in the nightlife scene downtown. From what Isla had heard of Axel's business affairs, sex, booze, and dealings with Otherworlders through nightclubs downtown, he was a ruthless businessman. "Lilly, if you'll excuse me, I am going to step out for a moment for some air." Smiling with genuine affection Isla turned and walked out to the balcony, discarding the untouched drink.

The pull of the open air enticed her towards the balcony, away from the crowded ballroom, far enough away to clear her mind from the thoughts that filled her head. Exhausted, she leaned against the balcony railing and looked up at the pale face of the moon. The gentle light glistened across the lake like diamonds.

Then, a deep voice broke the peaceful silence, forcing her to stifle a jump: "Mesmerizing, isn't it?"

CHAPTER 7

For just one moment she'd wanted to be alone. Just one.

The smell of tobacco danced through the air. Her gaze stayed fixed on the landscape, "It is."

"A false sense of freedom." The gentleman walked up to the balcony ledge next to Isla, with a smoke in one hand and a crystal glass in the other.

Even though his company was unwelcome, she disagreed with him. "That's false…Out here lie no boundaries, unlike in there where one can't help *feeling trapped.*" Trapped by an unwanted arranged mating. By not being able to escape people's annoying thoughts in a large crowd. The gathering was supposed to be a celebration of the union between two packs. Instead, she felt lost and alone, unsure of what step to take next in her journey.

Bourbon went down smooth as he contemplated the idea of feeling trapped. How could someone like her know what it was to be trapped? He looked at her. The moonlight highlighted Isla's outer beauty. Her light caramel blonde hair radiated as hints of gold glittered in the light. Her hazel eyes and soft pink lips were mesmerizing and he could not take his eyes off of her. All he could see was perfection, someone who didn't need to work for much. She couldn't possibly know what feeling trapped was. He did. Trapped. The thought of her feeling trapped irritated him. "In there is…security. Control. Out there…" he continued, looking past Isla, "beauty lures young pretty little things like you into a darkness from which you will not return."

Isla cautiously took his hand that was resting on the balcony railing into hers, turning it over as she looked at him. A light tingle of electricity danced across both of their bodies as she touched him, forcing him to tear his gaze from the darkness back to her. He was dangerous, tall, and had a darkness about him that was unnervingly intriguing to her. Her playful, light touch pulled at him as he leaned in towards her.

The sweet caramel notes of the bourbon mixed with the scent of the smoke as it danced through the air. There was something about this man that drew her away from the ledge to meet his gaze. "What does a guy with soft skin and expensive taste know about what lurks in the shadows?" A dark smile graced his face in amusement and his eyes softened. His eyes drank in every inch of her. He stopped when he saw the whip delicately wrapped around her wrist like an expensive bracelet. Slowly his finger traced over the whip. Deadly little thing she was.

"What is a beauty like you doing out here alone, talking to a stranger in the dark?" Isla took a guarded step back as she pulled her hand back from his touch. "Is there not enough entertainment in there? Miss Lilly would be quite displeased knowing someone wasn't enjoying themselves." He raised an eyebrow as he watched Isla shift uncomfortably, "I've been told, on the other hand, that I can be quite... *entertaining*. Pleasurable in fact." His silky deep voice drew her eyes back to his.

He reached to brush her soft, silky hair out of her face. His fingers traced the side of her neck as he dropped his hand. A trail of electricity tingled as his fingers touched her skin, causing her heart to race faster. "A party of two. Just you, me, and endless positions––I mean possibilities." His smile softened as he waited for his invitation to be accepted. One word, just one word and he would make this a night she would not forget.

This shocked her out of her reverie, "Says the conceited stranger. Does this talk often work on women you've just met to lure them into a dark corner only to fuck them and leave them in the cold?"

A playful laugh escaped him. "Yes. But usually, there is less talking and more fucking." Pressing her lips tightly together, Isla cautiously watched him while keeping space between them. The last thing she needed was someone seeing her too close, too friendly with another guy on the night she was meeting Axel, her future mate.

A silent tension stretched between them for a moment before it was broken by a ringing sound inside, calling people to gather around the stage. "Ah, what a shame." He turned toward the door as he waved his hand out in front of him. "After you." Like a gentleman, he opened the door for Isla as she walked back into reality. As the doors closed behind her, the soft, beautiful moonlit night was replaced by bright decorative ballroom chandeliers.

Winston summoned Isla to come stand beside him. She could feel he was displeased with her. Sneaking off. Hiding. It was the opposite of what he had told her to do tonight: *Be social, but not too social with the Griffiths.* A small rush of adrenalin warmed her body when she realized her flirt with danger had gone unnoticed. If he even suspected what had happened, he would be much more disapproving.

The mating is not final until the next wolf moon when you are mated. You need to show you are a worthy mate. The night was young, so she shrugged it off. She had time to make her Alpha proud of her. Part of her wondered what future would be possible if the Griffiths decided not to continue with the courtship for the arranged mating. Then, she quickly dismissed the thought, knowing this was the only outcome her Alpha wanted.

CHAPTER 8

Lilly began to thank her guests for coming and started to talk about the present and the future of their pack. Unexpectedly, Isla felt her skin shiver in warning, causing her to stand up straight and on alert. Slowly she scanned the room.

"Relax," Winston commanded her in a whisper.

Keeping her voice low she said, "Something is off." Isla hated being around so many people. It was hard to concentrate. But there was something in the air she could not make out.

Smiling, Winston gave her hand a reassuring pat. "It's just your nerves." When she quickly focused on his thoughts, Isla realized that he too felt uncomfortable at the large gathering of strangers without his pack. Being dependent on others was not in his character. This was supposed to have been a small gathering for the soon-to-be-mated couple to get acquainted with one another, but it had ended up being an egregiously overwhelming event.

Taking a deep breath, Isla tried to refocus on Lilly's speech. She wondered if Axel had any say in the arranged mating, or if he, like her, was powerless.

She put on a smile as Lilly welcomed her honored guests and personal friends.

Then she locked eyes with Selene, Lilly's daughter, who smiled directly at Isla as she stood next to Lilly, full of life and excitement. *About time Axel was mated. I am so excited to have a sister. He'd better not mess this up.* She was beautiful and charismatic. Isla couldn't help but return her smile and nod in her direction.

Garrett, on the other hand, was all but smiling. Next to his radiant wife and daughter, his gaze, which was fixed on Isla, was completely impassive. He was studying her. His stare was intense, but she didn't let it bother her. The tingle still pulled at her senses as she cautiously looked at the guests within her peripheral view. The entire crowd was captivated by Lilly as she spoke.

Front and center stood her mystery man from the balcony with a refreshed glass of bourbon. Displeased, she narrowed her eyes as she looked right at him. Had she not been on the balcony, what were the chances he would have found a needy, desperate female who would have given into his seductive ways? From the looks of the crowd, more than one woman was disappointed that Axel was taken and any one of them would have lifted her dress for him. He looked back at her with a lack of emotion that mirrored Garrett's expression. Not giving anything away. As Lilly finished introducing her son, he quickly downed his drink.

So, this is the famous Axel.

"Our first dance of the night, in honor of a prosperous future." Lilly raised her glass to the room and led the toast. As Isla did not have time to grab a drink for the toast, she smiled and nodded. As the band began to play, Axel walked over to Isla and handed his glass off to a member of the wait staff.

"Princess, may I have this dance?" Isla forced a smile when Winston cleared his throat and stepped aside. Nodding, she followed Axel's lead. All eyes were on them as they graced the dance floor. A spark tingled between their hands as they touched, just as it had before.

Following his lead, she listened to the music but continued to look over his shoulder at her surroundings, trying to ignore the energy that tingled between them. "Do you ever relax and just let go?"

She looked up at him. His eyes were captivating. Dark and mysterious. A little glassy from drinking. "Not really, no."

"What has you so on edge? Even out on the balcony, you were

rigid." He twirled her and she gracefully followed his lead. *How I could loosen you up?* "You need a strong drink," *for starters.*

"Alcohol dulls the senses."

Laughing, he agreed. "Hence why you need a double. There is nothing to be on guard for. Just relax and have a good time. It is a party, after all." *Goddess knows I need another drink to get through tonight.*

Music flowed through the room with them as other couples started to join the dance floor. Axel kept a light hold on her waist and his eyes locked on hers. She could feel people looking at them, but she didn't care. Instead, Isla focused on the beautiful notes of the music as she started to relax in Axel's hold. Her black and purple iridescent dress shimmered as they moved gracefully as one to the music.

When his free hand slowly traveled down her exposed back, a tingled trailed under his touch. Did he feel this too? Looking up into his eyes, she saw they were softer than before. More seductive, enchanting. Her pulse accelerated as she felt a flutter of excitement in her stomach. For a moment she was lost in him, as if no one else existed. Blushing, she broke eye contact. Though he carefully maintained his emotionless poker face, Axel liked the way she responded to his touch.

Twirling her out to arm's length, Axel enjoyed the full view of Isla's elegant gliding and moving of her body. Isla smirked as she noticed a brief break in his eyes as he looked at her and pulled her back into a very close, intimate position, closing the space between their bodies. His hand cupped the small of her lower back. He captured her gaze once more and said, "This was unexpected."

Gorgeous. Good dancer. Great body. Isla listened to his thoughts, a superficial checklist. Knowing his reputation, his thoughts didn't surprise her.

He continued to search her face, as he tried to read her. "Do you not find me intriguing, Princess?"

As much as she wanted to scold him for his behavior on the balcony, she kept a fake smile painted on her face as she narrowed her eyes only for him to see. "Why, I do find you intriguing." An arrogant smile graced his face. "I find it intriguing how just a few moments ago you were trying to seduce a stranger into a dark corner before meeting me for our gathering."

Another seductive laugh escaped him. Not many people made him laugh. Her thick sarcasm only made him more interested in her. "Tried. But didn't." Ignoring the rolling of her eyes, he continued, "The way I remember it, it was just a thought––it's not like I actually tried to seduce you."

"One and the same."

He pulled her completely against his body. As he bent down to whisper in her ear, his breath sent a wave of warmth through her body. "Princess, you would know if I tried to seduce you. We wouldn't be here still. Let alone be standing." Axel smelled the desire that rolled off of her. He smiled as the sweet scent of her arousal danced in the air around him.

"You are inappropriate." Deflecting his comments, she tried to hide what she felt, but her scent didn't lie.

"I've been called worse and you smell of..."

CHAPTER 9

A scream sliced through the air like a shock wave. With her body still pressed against Axel's, she heard the commotion before she could focus on where it was coming from. Chaos broke out after the first scream echoed through the ballroom. A void slammed into her head. A Crazed.

Isla quickly turned her head toward the source of the void. Shit. Isla swiftly moved her leg between Axel's as she knocked him off balance and swept his leg out from under him. Axel kept a hold of Isla as they fell to the ground. Isla fell on top of him as a dagger flew past them and hit a bystander.

"Normally I'm the one on top with a sweet thing like you melting underneath me."

Screams rang through her head. Baffled, "This is what you are thinking of in a time like this?"

"I'm always thinking about--"

Another scream ripped through Isla's ears. She closed her eyes for a moment to quiet her panicked thoughts, she needed to focus. When she opened her eyes, she looked up to assess her surroundings. Adrenaline surged through her as she saw a Crazed cornering Lilly, who was completely unarmed. "Stay down and out of my way." Before he could respond, Isla jumped up off of Axel. She grasped the enchanted whip around her wrist to free it. The whip elongated from a delicate bracelet to a deadly weapon and it shimmered in the light.

Axel watched her spring into action, moving gracefully through the panicked guests who ran for safety. She was sexy as she wielded the long whip that was as flexible as her body. It wasn't a bad sight from where Axel was laying. Not a bad sight at all.

Without wasting any time, Isla threw the end of the deadly whip through the air. It wrapped around the Crazed's neck and yanked him backward. When she pulled the whip back, it snapped his neck and he dropped dead. Two more Crazed turned towards Lilly and Isla. Their black, dark, predator eyes filled with death and fixated on their prey.

Isla moved between Lilly and the Crazed. "Stay behind me." Adrenaline continued to surge through her as she watched the Crazed continue their attack. A screeching sound pierced through the screams of the crowd. She pulled her whip around before flicking her wrist. The whip soared through the air and slashed the first Crazed, dropping him to the ground. A gunshot exploded in the air as the second Crazed dropped dead next to her with another screech.

She looked up from the direction of the gunshot. Axel kept a poised aim and winked at her.

Isla stood in front of Lilly to ensure no other Crazed came close to her. The Griffiths' security had quickly neutralized the remaining Crazed, but many were still on edge. Screams slowly dissolved into a hum of talk. Lilly was overwhelmed with emotion. Howling from several of the warriors in the room brought everyone's attention to Garrett and Winston, who were covered in blood.

Garrett walked over to Lilly, looking her over to ensure she was unharmed before embracing her affectionately. Then he turned to Isla saying, "Thank you. You are more than worthy to be a part of my family." He kissed the top of Lilly's head and kept her tucked under his arm in a secure hold. "You both will learn that a mate is the most important thing in life. One's reason to live. To even breathe. She is everything to me."

Garrett turned to the room, keeping Lilly under his arm and against his body. The carnage of the Crazed and a few victims laid lifeless on the floor. The beautiful white, blue, silver, and yellow decorations and flowers and white marble floors were now covered in dark red blood. A few wounded were being helped to the infirmary. Many of the remaining guests had fled the room which was now contained by the security team. Any humans that were present would have their memories erased before leaving, replacing what they saw with only memories of a good party filled with drinking and dancing.

"Shadow Warriors, we will meet in the war room to debrief. Winston and Isla, you will also join us." This was not a request.

Axel closed the space between them as he secured his gun in the holster on his back. Hearing his Father publicly announce he accepted Isla made everything real. He thought that—considering the events from tonight with the attack on their pack, an attack in their own home— this would not be the time to entertain the ridiculous idea that he should be mated. Sure, he had felt the chemistry outside and she was kind on the eyes—the thought of taking her to his bed had definitely crossed his mind—but he had never considered the possibility that his father was serious about the mating.

Isla felt her body respond to Axel as he approached her, it wanted him near. The experience was new and she was uncomfortable with how it made her feel. She held her breath as Axel leaned in close to her ear. "If you had any hope of being freed from our mating, you just lost it."

Isla secured her whip around her arm and it formed back into a bracelet trying, as she tried to keep her eyes off of him. "Maybe you shouldn't have shot the Crazed then." At least then her future would have been determined by fate. She let her eyes glance up to meet his.

"Ah come on now Princess. Where would the fun in that be?"

Winston walked over to Axel and nodded to him. "You have good aim."

Axel kept his eyes locked with Isla's. "I never miss." His confidence could have been mistaken for arrogance. She wondered how much truth there was to his deadly aim. Axel left without another word.

CHAPTER 10

Axel took a long, hot shower. Then he slammed the door to his bathroom behind him before he paced around his room getting ready for *his* pack's meeting with *his* Alpha. What was his father thinking, inviting Isla and her Alpha to come along? They were not part of their pack. There was nothing for them to debrief on or contribute to.

Frustration boiled in his veins. He sure as hell did not think his father would actually commit to the mating. The gathering was supposed to be for show. The idea had been to string along their pack until they were able to assess where the war was heading. Instead, he had acted in the heat of the moment, forging an actual commitment Axel did not want. Not right now anyway. He had so much going on with his business, he did not need this complication.

He had planned to stay hidden on the balcony until he was required to make an appearance. Alone. Away from her. His hand ran through his hair. The moment the light breeze had carried her scent to them, it had enticed him. It had pulled him to her. As he closed his eyes, he could almost smell her all over again.

Axel knew it was her when he saw her standing on the balcony. Moonlight framed her silhouette in the darkness as if the Moon Goddess herself was drawing her. She looked perfect. Smelled amazing. At first, he thought about seducing her and using her behavior as a weapon to end the mating ritual, to free himself of the unwanted distraction. The moment she touched his hand and he felt the electricity prickle on his skin, however, it drew his beast out. He would not allow his father to use her like that again.

A harsh knock on his bedroom door broke him out of his thoughts and he said, "Enter."

His Alpha walked in. "Son."

"Father." Axel composed himself, straightening his posture.

Garrett walked around the room, looking at the mess Axel made. His disappointment in Axel needed no words. Axel was used to the look. Silence stretched between them as he waited until he was spoken to.

"Tonight was meant to be an important night. I had specifically told you what I expected of you." Axel listened, not saying a word even though he had plenty to say. "You completely disobeyed my instructions. You were not even present at your own gathering ceremony. People noticed. I noticed. You were supposed to act like you were getting to know her. Instead, you were holed off in a corner drinking yourself to death. Doing the exact opposite of what I told you to do."

Technically he had still been there, just outside. And he had not technically been in a corner. "So little faith in me. I found my opportunity to...what did you say, *get to know her* on the balcony."

Garrett snapped his head around towards Axel and closed the space between them in one swift step out of anger. "Do not mock me, boy. Had you been on point at the gathering...inside...maybe you would have noticed the fucking Crazed."

So now the Crazed infiltrating his security was his fault? It was so easy for his Alpha to pass the blame. Cautiously, Axel engaged with his father. "How so many Crazed were able to get past security unnoticed I still cannot wrap my head around." Crazed had an odor of death that an Otherworlder would not miss, let alone a pack of highly skilled warriors. "Father, with the new turn of events, perhaps now is not the time to move forward with the arranged mating."

Garrett hit Axel across the face. "Wake up! You did not stick to the plan. Instead, *she* stepped up––forcing my hand." Taking a deep breath Garrett calmed himself before continuing. "One day you will be the Alpha of this pack. In a time of war breaking on the horizon, you will have to choose which side you will be on. Every decision you make must be calculated. If you cannot handle the decisions and sacrifices, then you will not be the next Alpha, and that is final." Axel stared at his father as the words hit him. The only ways in which someone else would succeed Garrett, was if Axel was dead or if he relinquished his position by a challenge from another bloodline.

As the door closed behind Garrett, Axel flexed the hands he had fisted by his side.

CHAPTER 11

Clean and dressed in comfortable clothes, Isla joined the Shadow Pack in their war room. She was impressed with the state-of-the-art technology of their operations center. It was more sophisticated than anything they had back at her pack.

As she took a seat in the back of the room against the wall she watched as all of the pack members in the room took their places around the very large table. The males were all muscular and stocky. How they had fit into a tuxedo earlier in the evening was beyond Isla. Size was not always everything. It definitely was an advantage in a fight, a Werewolf fight, but being skilled in weaponry was also an advantage.

Isla's Midnight Pack believed in training all their warriors in tactical combat––not just bare knuckles and guns. No, males in her pack were trained in weaponry, to be able to use any object as a weapon––survival. There was such a thing as being too big. Too much muscle. It made you too heavy, resulting in slower movement. Though when she assessed the way they carried themselves, she was sure they were still deadly fast.

Axel, who leaned against the wall near Isla, pointed to her wrist as he said, "Do you really need to wear *that*? There's no threat of danger here."

She returned his scowl with a steady gaze of her own. "I never take it off. *Ever.*" After holding his gaze for a moment she added, "And the threat assessment is still out."

Garrett started the meeting by reviewing their security plan.

Different members around the room were asked to report.

Someone in here fucked up and I want their head. Garrett's anger was radiating from his body, she didn't need to read his thoughts to know he was livid.

I checked guests and the lists multiple times. Security was all in position. No way a bunch of Crazed could've just walked up unnoticed. The pack member with glasses was nervous as hell as he waited until Garrett turned to him.

Looking around the room, Isla noticed she was one of the only females in the all-boys club, it was just her and Lilly. Her eyes came to rest on the wall, where she could see dozens of screens replaying security footage from the estate. Footage of guests being checked outside the door being greeted played. Invitations were being checked. Drowning out the anxious thoughts of the men in the room, Isla started looking for signs of the Crazed arriving.

Axel watched Isla with curiosity. His intense stare teased her to look at him, but she refused to give in. She forced herself to keep her eyes on the screen. *What could she possibly be able to find that the entire team of highly trained security professionals couldn't?*

"There. Stop the footage." The entire room went silent and everyone stared at her. "Back up the tape 30 seconds. Stop. That is the Crazed who attacked Lilly. If you look for the ones your warriors can remember neutralizing, your security team will probably be able to identify who they saw as a regular guest."

Easy for her to make something like this up. The bodies have since dissolved into piles of dust. How convenient for her. Duke, Garrett's second in command, was anything but impressed with Isla.

Crickets could be heard as everyone continued to stare at her—saying nothing but making up for it in thought. First of all, no one ever interrupted Garrett, let alone during a debrief. Secondly, she was not part of their pack—what gave her the right to even speak? Isla and Winston were only part of the meeting out of respect between Alphas.

Winston gave her a disapproving look for speaking out. He didn't need to say anything to her, his look said it all. Isla wanted to crawl under the table, but she held her head high in confidence, even if her Alpha wasn't supporting her.

Lilly was the first to break the unnerving silence with her soft, gentle voice. "She's right." She looked up at Garrett before looking back at the frozen screen as she continued, "That is the Crazed that nearly attacked me, had it not been for Isla and her quick thinking." Lilly's voice was shaky. Garrett placed a hand on her shoulder as he stood behind her, comforting her. Garrett trusted his mate unconditionally. He nodded, registering the information.

"Now we know how they got in. But how the hell did they even get this close in the first place? And how were they not detected? None of this makes sense. Not one pack member picked up the Crazeds' scent. Not one! What makes matters worse is that these Crazed were in control of themselves!" His voice tapered off as he let this truth sink in. The Crazed were controlled by blood lust and yet they had blended into the party undetected, waiting to attack. This was bad. Really bad.

The room broke out, scrutinizing who had messed up and allowed this to happen. No answers. Just blame. Speculation. Garrett slammed his hand down on the desk silencing everyone. "Isla, what is your take?"

Duke cut in before Isla could speak, "Garrett, *her*? Shouldn't we hear from the security team that was on the ground during the attack?" Duke's dark features were haunting.

"No one here has given me anything tangible thus far. All I've heard are excuses from your team."

Duke's eyes shot daggers at Isla before looking back at Garrett. "But she's an outsider."

Garret narrowed his eyes at this clear act of defiance. "Exactly. I want to hear a different perspective from someone who's not trying to cover their own ass. Because right now, I'm ready to tear into everyone who failed at their mission tonight, starting with *you*."

His long black, straight hair and dark insightful eyes shifted back to Isla.

This bitch better watch herself. He's lost his damn mind thinking my team failed at their duty. Probably wants to test the goods before Axel mates her, putting on a show like this.

Taking a deep breath, Isla focused on the screens, trying not to let the gravity of the situation weigh on her. "The Crazed were able to get through security undetected."

Duke's fury hit her like a tidal wave. "What? You trying to say this is my fucking fault? What the fuck do you know?"

Garrett threw Duke a silencing glance before turning back to Isla.

Duke's emotional outburst sent a warning Axel did not like. He stopped leaning against the wall and stood up straight.

Isla stood up too. She felt trapped and small sitting down in front of everyone. Phrasing her words carefully she said, "That is not what I am saying or implying. To an outsider, your parties and gatherings are well-known. You host guests for a variety of occasions throughout the year, to form or maintain relationships." Garrett nodded his agreement. Nothing she was saying was earth-shattering. "The responsibility of hosting gatherings with a wide range of Otherworlders is complicated I'm sure––and a lot of thought goes into every detail."

Duke was skeptical about where Isla was going with her analysis. *She's been here for a couple of hours and she acts like knows everything. She'll be put in her place soon enough if she doesn't watch her step. This ain't the woods. She's Red Riding Hood and I'm the Big Bad fucking Wolf who is going to have her for lunch.*

Isla struggled to keep her focus on Garrett with Duke's thoughts burning in the back of her mind, causing her a headache. "I can tell you from my visit today that security was present. Both those in plain view to be noticed by guests and those who were assigned to blend in. Even with the Crazed breaching security, your team neutralized the threat quickly."

Not quickly enough. But that will be dealt with. Garrett needed no words to express his thoughts.

"This is the first gathering I've attended. However, I would wonder, are the same protocols in place for every event?"

Duke jumped up and kicked his chair back against the wall, "Of course they are." Garrett was becoming visibly irritated with Duke's emotional outbursts as he motioned for him to take a seat. Isla didn't notice Axel taking a protective step closer to her. He was intrigued with what Isla had to say, but more suspicious as to why Duke was acting out. The Wolf within him was quickly becoming agitated with Duke's reaction, cautiously watching, feeling a need to be close to Isla. To protect her if it came to that. If Duke lost control, Axel's beast was ready to attack.

Winston waved his hand as he signaled for her to continue cautiously.

"I would then wonder if someone would be able to study your protocols and routines. I'm not sure how many gatherings you host during a year but if someone had been observing, taking notes, learning the ins and outs, could it be possible? I would suspect this was a trial run for what is to come."

The room broke out into chatter about who could be the source of the plan. One warrior raised his voice above the buzz, saying, " A failed plan, at that." Many of the warriors grunted in agreement.

Garrett cleared his throat to quiet the room so Isla could finish her observations. "It would depend on what the mission was. If the plan was to mark and take out a target then you are correct." The memory of the dagger flying past her and Axel as they fell to the ground resurfaced. "If the plan was to infiltrate and draw out your warriors who were on assigned duties, testing you, testing your response, I would say it was not a complete loss."

Smart. Sexy. And can handle a weapon, Axel thought. *Being forced into an arranged mating with Isla may have its perks after all. As* he leaned in to whisper in her ear, Isla felt the warmth on Axel's breath, "First you lose any chance of getting out of the pre-arranged mating. Now you speak like you out-rank almost everyone in this room and seal your alliance to the Shadow Pack, all in one day. Your reputation precedes you, Princess."

"All coming from a guy who spends his time wheeling and dealing with low-life Otherworlders in nightclubs and hasn't been on the front lines of a battlefield once. Drugs, sex, and, wait... more sex. Did I miss anything? Your reputation precedes you as well."

Axel glanced up to focus on the conversation taking place in the room. Clearly, he was not needed. He had not even been acknowledged in the room by his Alpha.

CHAPTER 12

Tonight had not turned out the way Axel had anticipated. He had thought that by this time he would be in his bedroom having a nightcap with one or two very willing, very sexy ladies, privately celebrating his freedom. Instead, he was forced to escape to the one place in which he had complete control: his club. As he walked up to the VIP area, he grabbed a bottle and a glass from behind the bar. A dark corner called his name as he walked past his VIP guests, ignoring some ladies' poor attempts to get his attention.

As quickly as the first glass was filled, he downed his drink. The alcohol hit him like a train. Not eating earlier had probably been a mistake on his part, but he couldn't care less. Leaning back against the soft couch, he stretched out his legs and leaned his head back.

How could he have let this happen? He knew better than to screw around. He could not get Isla out of his thoughts. She was prettier than he expected. Scratch that she was sexy. He had everything under control until she touched his hand. That touch, the electricity, he had never felt anything like it.

His beast whimpered inside, wanting more of whatever happened between them tonight. The way she felt against his body on the dance floor. Shit, the way she handled herself with her whip was a turn-on. The girl was an actual Goddess.

He closed his eyes and tried to think of what he'd do with Isla. What he would do with her body. Her hands. Her lips. A soft groan sounded in the back of his throat as he pictured Isla.

Deep in thought and almost drunk, his peaceful moment was broken by the feeling of a woman grabbing his shoulders as she mounted his lap. His eyes opened and he couldn't help but feel entirely unimpressed with Cami who should be working, attending to his guests making him money.

"Axel, I didn't think you would come in tonight." Cami leaned down and kissed his lips, but he did not return the kiss.

Slumped against the couch he sat in his position, not moving, letting her do the work. "Oh, baby you don't look so good. Let me cheer you up." Cami continued planting kisses on his face and his neck. Like the blonde-haired, blue-eyed vixen she was, she turned her charm on to full blast and let her hands run down his chest to his pants. Still, he did not move or engage with her, though he didn't stop her either.

"Let me see what I am working with." She ran her hand up his inner thigh to his sex and felt nothing. "Hmm, maybe a little too much to drink, but I can fix this with ease."

The feeling of her hands working their way into his pants made his beast recoil. She was smoking hot, but his beast craved the touch of Isla––not this barely covered, fake Barbie doll desperate for attention.

Internally, he cursed at his Wolf. Then, before she could undo his belt buckle, Axel grabbed her hands.

"Shit!"

In one swift motion, he picked up Cami and placed her on the couch next to him. Without looking at her, Axel stood up and grabbed his bottle. As he headed to his office he let the door slam behind him.

Dropping in his chair behind his wooden desk, Axel set down the bottle and glass. The darkness of his office was welcomed. He didn't bother turning on any additional lights. The wall light was enough for him to function in his drunken state. Even though his eyesight was sharp in the dark, alcohol definitely dulled his senses. The thought made him smile, thinking of Isla.

Hearing the door open a few seconds after he just closed it only irritated him.

"What the hell, Axel!"

He was not in the mood to listen to her whiney voice. Ignoring her, he refilled his glass as she walked up to him, her black high heels clicking across his floor, pulling her lowcut top down further to expose her assets. Any further and they would pop out of her top.

"Baby, come on, let me take care of you." The feeling of her hand between his legs was anything but a turn-on.

Sighing, Axel grabbed her hand as he set his glass down. "Cami, enough. I am to be mated. You have a job to do, and that is to make me money. There are no more added bonuses or perks."

Shock and disbelief splashed over her face like a bucket of ice water. Her dark, smoky makeup made her bright blue angry eyes flare at him. Her thoughts were painted all over her face: what was going on? He had never rejected her advances. They had always had good sex... Confused and hurt, she turned around. As she reached the door Axel's voice caught her, "And next time, knock before you come into my office."

CHAPTER 13

Isla looked out the window. Sunlight broke the horizon, filling the dawn with golden rays glistening across the land. Last night seemed like a whirlwind. She was still trying to make sense of it all. It was obvious someone or something was not in favor of the mating between the Midnight and Shadow Packs. But their efforts had only sealed the deal. Any hope of returning to her former life, to her independence, was now gone.

Last night, Garrett officially approved the mating and alliance between the packs, making Isla feel shackled and confined. Mixed emotions tangled up in her like vines. Part of her knew her arranged mating and the alliance it brought to her pack was much needed. Regardless, the pressure of the situation weighed on her. The survival of her pack and The Realm relied on Isla not making a mistake. Ever. There was no rule book to guide her. Her parents were gone. Her grandfather was focused on her mating process, obsessed almost. Today, everything felt different, more complicated. She needed to let out some steam.

Entering the training room, she felt a sense of calm. Here she could let loose without being judged on what kind of mate she would make. Worried about saying the wrong thing. Doing the wrong thing. Here she could let go of everything. At least temporarily.

The room was well organized with separate areas for weapons, obstacles, weights, simulation, and a sparring ring. This was much more sophisticated than what she was used to! The sounds of grunting brought her attention to the simulated training area.

Blades sliced through the air, each strike placed with force and precision. The sound was music to her ears. Axel's muscles flexed with intensity with each throw. Beads of sweat rolled down his skin. After each simulated attack, the opponents dropped one-by-one until the round was over. As he took a few deep breaths to slow his heart rate back down, he asked, "Do you like what you see Princess?" He kept his back to her, he didn't need to turn around to see who it was as he had picked up her scent as soon as she walked in.

Caught off guard, she said, "The training center is impressive, I will admit." She knew what he meant, but was not interested in going there with him. Axel kept his back to her as he toweled off some of his sweat. Heat radiated from him. Tribal tattoos covered his right shoulder and arm. The black tattoos were a fine work of art that had been hidden beneath his clothes last night.

Axel rumbled at her attempt to evade his inquisition but decided to let it slide. For now. "Not like home, is it?" When he turned around, she couldn't help but marvel at his masculinity. His ruggedness. Veins pulsing with raw energy. Skin glistening from his sweat. His eyes were intense as he turned around to look at her.

It was hard to find words when he looked at her like that. "Bigger––I mean your training center is state of the art." The sound of her nervous voice stirred his beast awake, wanting to play.

After a few moments of staring at her as if she was the next training course, she shifted uncomfortably. Something inside her awakened. Her eyes wandered down his shirtless all-male body.

"Well let's see what you got."

Isla snapped her attention back as she followed him over to the sparring area. "Take that off." He commanded her as he pointed down to her enchanted whip wrapped around her wrist.

Shaking her head, "I do not ever take this off. I'm quite good with it."

Smiling, he agreed, as he remembered how effective she had been last night with her whip slaying the Crazed. There was no denying she was deadly with it. She was good, but he also knew his request made her uncomfortable, which he found amusing. "You need to be prepared for any situation. You know, Princess, if you are more comfortable going over to the *beginner's* training area to practice, I won't stop you. It's probably safer so that you do not hurt yourself." Isla didn't know what bothered her more. His arrogance and dismissive tone, or the suggestion that she wasn't a match for him. Or that he kept calling her a *princess*, which she was not.

All her life she'd felt the need to prove her value, her worth to her pack. To always do things better than everyone else. From most, she had earned respect. Axel, on the other hand, needed a good ass whipping, which she could deliver no problem with her whip in hand. Axel wanting her to not use it, to take it off, made her feel awkward. She never fought without it.

Breaking his stare, he turned back to gather his workout gear. "That's what I thought."

Something inside her snapped. "Fine."

Axel turned around with a shit grin that said he had already won. He picked up her whip, tossed it behind him and sucker punched her in the stomach. Letting out a sharp gasp of air, she stumbled back a step. "You didn't say we were starting."

"First rule of combat, *people out in the real world don't play by the rules*. You have to be ready for anything." Axel knew he could have easily broken one of her ribs. His intention had not been to hurt her. At least, not too much. Maybe later she would let him tend to her body, inside and out. Again, Axel had to shake himself out of his reverie. Isla took the punch like a champ and gathered herself together with a deep breath. Axel patiently watched her body move as she shifted her weight between her feet.

Isla started throwing a few light jabs, which Axel blocked effortlessly. They each assessed each other's reflexes and speed as they moved through the sparring area, throwing jabs at each other.

Then, Axel changed up his rhythm and tried to sweep Isla's feet out from under her. She evaded the sweep and landed a solid punch to his jaw, followed by another jab. Throwing her weight into her first punch stung but she refused to show him she had anything but control. Her fists were clenched as she kept her focus on him, waiting for his next move.

After spitting out blood, Axel rubbed his jaw. Now, she was a worthy opponent. Game on.

As they continued to spar, the hits and kicks started getting heat behind them, each fighter calculating when to strike. A few pack members entered the training center for their morning workout and caught sight of Axel and Isla sparring. One-by-one the pack members gathered in the background, forming a small audience that watched the workout in progress.

The growing audience started exchanging hushed bets, guessing how long Isla could last in the ring. Isla drowned out the low murmur and instead concentrated on Axel, pushing the spectators' thoughts out of her head. No one questioned who would win this bout. Axel was a skilled warrior with Alpha blood. He was bigger and faster than Isla. Plus, they all noticed she didn't have her whip. Had she had her whip, they would be taking very different bets.

People out in the real world don't play by the rules. As much as Isla wanted to prove to herself she could go toe-to-toe with Axel and hold her own, part of her wanted to win and prove that she wasn't a bitch to be messed with.

She changed her pace and moved in for a take-down. The minute he landed on the mat near the side, Isla spun around to reach for her whip on the opposite end of the sparring area.

However, this was when Axel's impeccable male Werewolf instincts kicked in. Isla's going for her enchanted whip gave Axel enough time to reach for a training gun and shoot a practice dart at her. Upon impact, a small pinch of red die oozed out. Isla hardly noticed it as she twirled around, ready to unleash her fury.

Stunned, she looked at him still holding the practice gun pointed at her.

"I won, princess. Lesson two, don't be so desperate to go for the obvious. And don't turn your back on the enemy."

Confused and flustered she scolded him. "What? You shot me? In the back! The gun was not part of this."

Smiling, he tossed the gun off to the side and started to reach for his water bottle and towel. Either it was the feeling of losing to someone who played dirty or wanting to take a play out of his playbook, charged with emotions, Isla sent out her whip grabbing his arm. As she pulled on her whip to turn him to face her she landed one last punch across his face and kicked him to the ground. Before he could say anything, she spat out, "Now the match is over. And I'm no fucking princess." Heat rolled off her body as she stormed out of the room––without acknowledging the audience. Low whistles danced around the sparring ring. She was a damn force to be reckoned with.

CHAPTER 14

Duke broke up the chatter as he walked over to Axel, who was still laying on the ground with a grin on his face. Duke was less than amused. "I don't know what's worse. That I have to report to your father that you tried to kick her ass, or that you let a female land you flat on your back. What the hell were you thinking? She could have gotten seriously hurt. And that..."

Axel's smile faded as he got up to cut Duke off. The last thing he needed was a lecture from Duke. "And what? You saw how she handled herself last night. I didn't dish out anything she couldn't take. I knew she would go for her whip. I was waiting to see if she would use it."

"And what are the others supposed to think?" Glancing around the room, Duke vaguely motioned to the few pack members and some of the female staff who had started their morning workouts.

"Why should I give a shit what other people think?"

Duke ran his hand through his hair, damning the courtship visit for what was not the first time. "You're supposed to be setting an example. I don't need people going around and acting like idiots here. And *she* is supposed to be setting an example to fit in, build relationships within our pack. How is your little session supposed to help that? Huh? How are the other females going to accept her as one of their own if she is acting like a warrior? Shit, next thing I know I am going to have to start training girls." To Duke, females were the weaker part of the species: They did not shift to a Werewolf form, and they were not as strong as the males. To him, they were good for sex and serving the pack to breed offspring.

There were talented and skilled females in the pack who could make great warriors. But tradition said that they were meant to hold other roles, none of which were on the front line. A select few worked their way to security detail or intel, but never in special ops or actual combat. "How much do you really care whether she is successful at fitting in here?" Axel didn't wait for a response before leaving Duke in the training center. He wasn't the alpha of the pack. Axel would see to it he never would be.

Once he became Alpha, he would see to it Duke was removed from his position. He had never liked Duke; he didn't trust him. His father had given the man way too much freedom to make decisions on his own. Too much power. Unchecked power was dangerous. Duke did not value female Werewolves or anyone else he felt beneath him.

To Axel, the females of their bloodline were precious. They were their greatest hope of having strong, purebred males who were like no other species. What's more, mating made the male stronger. There was nothing deadlier than a mated male whose female was in danger. A mated male would stop at nothing to protect his female.

Breeding was important for their survival, as it was for most of the Otherworlder species. The elite and royal bloodlines had to be kept strong so that they were not overthrown. The fittest survived. The strongest ruled.

It has been over a century since two predominant packs had arranged a mating between families. Ever since twelve dangerous Crazed Otherworlders had broken out of the Underground, species of all races had been on alert. Strategic alliances, training, and strengthening their forces had been the top priority. Winston Bane and Garrett Griffith had seen smaller wars for power among their race. But the situation right now was nothing like any of the elders had ever seen. A storm was brewing like a hurricane. Fear stimulated the need for change to ensure survival for their future.

Even though Axel was not keen on his Alpha making the decision to commit to the arranged mating, he understood the weight of the situation. At least she could hold her own. He had never met anyone like her. No female had ever stood up to him before today. A smile graced his lips as he thought how easy it was to get under her skin. She had a sexy, dangerous side to her that he found to be a complete turn-on.

CHAPTER 15

Winston sat across from his granddaughter in her room, glaring at her. After taking a long, hot shower, her muscles started to relax from the stiffness she felt when she moved. Bruises were hidden beneath her clothes, hidden from his wandering, judging eyes. They would heal soon enough. Having Werewolf blood running through her had its advantages. She wouldn't heal as fast as a male Werewolf, but still faster than a human.

"This is not how you should be acting." Her grandfather looked beyond disappointed with Isla. And she didn't have to read his thoughts to know what he was thinking. Before they'd left their pack house and came to the Griffiths' estate, he had been clear with her on how she needed to make the mating her priority. Her only priority. It was her duty to represent her pack well, to ensure the mating process was completed. They would be blood bonded by the next wolf moon, after all. The gathering was just the beginning of the courtship, though, and she still had a long way to go to ensure the mating was secured. Garrett approved of Isla last night, but she needed to keep his approval.

Winston knew of Axel's reputation. He was much like his father had been at his age. The difference was that Garrett had needed Lilly's mating, as the pack had needed financial resources to embark on different business ventures. Now, the Shadow pack was thriving and financially sound. It was not in need of financial resources, training, or warriors. The only thing they gained by the mating was the alliance between the packs and the Midnight pack's connection to The Realm.

Preparing for war meant making strategic alliances.

Exhausted, she didn't have the energy to debate with him. Instead, she cut straight to the point. "Act how? Act like a warrior like I am? Act like the protector of The Realm I am?" In just a few days he had shifted from being proud and encouraging her to be the best she could be to lead the pack, to now...something else. Something she was unfamiliar with. Everything she did, lately, was either wrong or not to his liking. She was disappointing.

"You are going to be mated to Axel. The mating between the Midnight Pack and Shadow Pack is needed for us to survive the test of time. Your duty..."

"Yes, I know. My duty to the pack, to The Realm, exceeds all others." Isla had lost count of how many times she had heard him say that.

"Your *duty* to the pack and The Realm means being a leader who will provide safety to those who cannot protect themselves. To ensure our bloodline lives on and thrives." His heartfelt words were the first honest feelings she'd heard from her grandfather since they'd been on this trip. "Your parents understood their duty to ensure the survival of the pack. They gave the pack a strong woman who would bring security with her mating." Just as quickly as the heartfelt comments had brought sentiment and reassurance, the reminder that she was his property was a slap in the face. How she wished her mother was here to guide her.

Isla didn't know the first thing about being courted in an arranged mating. How to act. How to look. What to say. Let alone what was expected of her. With people like the Griffiths, appearance was everything. Why was being who you are so wrong and frowned upon? Why would being a strong, independent leader not be favored in a time of war? None of this made sense to her. "What do you want me to do?" The question slipped out in a defeated, compliant tone. Acting of her own volition was not wanted. Property had value. A pawn was moved strategically in a game of chess. With each move, the strategy changed to ensure a win.

With a sigh of relief, Winston started to put the next part of his plan in motion, "Nothing is guaranteed until the mating is done. You need to form relationships in the pack, especially with Axel and his family. Become part of his world. Whatever it takes."

"And how do you suggest I do that?" He obviously had plans already set in place for her.

His smile acknowledged her compliance and the hold he still had over her. No love. Just the satisfaction of her obedience. "I've already arranged for you to go out with Selene."

"What am I supposed to do with Selene?" They were nothing alike. She doubted they would have anything in common. Isla had her duty and responsibilities. Selene, from what she could tell, from the few interactions they had had, was anything but responsible. A free spirit who did what she wanted and loved attention.

CHAPTER 16

'Fit in', he had said. 'Be one of the girls' and most of all, 'be likable'. Winston didn't say she had to get Selene to like her, he had told her to be likable. His obsession with Isla's mating was all he focused on. Not once since they had arrived at the Shadow Pack's territory had he asked how she was doing, not even after the attack. Things were different now.

Staring at another shot placed in front of her at the bar, Isla thought that if they kept this pace up, they might as well be drinking from the bottle. Then, she started thinking about how much she missed her mom. Selene was too busy socializing and talking to everyone around her to notice Isla nursing the shot. How easy it would be to just go with it and drown her worries for one night. To let go and just stop being her. Though the escape would only be temporary, the thought was very tempting.

The hustle and bustle of the bar patrons was a blur. "Cheers!" Forcing a smile, Isla nodded but only sipped her shot. Frowning, Selene bounced over and took a seat next to Isla. "You're not having fun, are you?"

Isla shrugged, "It's not that." Selene was trying to be nice the only way she knew how. "It's just been a long week." Lightening up her tone she continued, "You seem to know everyone here."

Her bright smile returned to her face. "Of course I do. O-M-G. You probably don't know, but this is one of Axel's clubs. Anyone who is anyone in the Underground--well anyone worth knowing--goes here. And there's the occasional human circles that come in along with random visitors." Selene turned and started pointing out cliques that were regulars. She was in on all the latest gossip.

Isla found herself looking around. She could sense Axel was somewhere in the club as the tingle on her back when he touched her during their dance came alive. Finally, she spotted him standing in the VIP area, making his rounds among staff and exclusive guests. The waitresses dressed in barely anything, more like lingerie, made their way around serving guests. One of them stopped next to Axel. Isla couldn't help but notice how flirty the blonde bombshell was with him. Axel was hard to read, but Isla remembered her from the party. For being staff, she was awfully friendly with the boss. That, she didn't like.

Axel could feel Isla's eyes on him. She had an unmistakable scent he could recognize anywhere. But he ignored her, he had business to take care of.

"Ugh." Selene saw who Isla was looking at. "Don't worry about her, she's old news." But Selene's thoughts said something a bit different: *She'd better be old news. Axel told me he ended it.*

Sometimes Isla's gift was a nuisance. Sometimes, she wished she was normal and not cursed. Trying to play innocent she said, "What do you mean *old* news?"

For the first time, Selene was momentarily speechless. As much as she loved attention and being the center of everything, she was not one to cross a line with Axel and cause any issues. Quickly, she changed the subject, "Hey, you didn't finish your shot!"

Isla retorted, "And you didn't answer my question." As she looked back up at Axel, he locked eyes with her and headed down from the VIP level after speaking with one of his security guards. Isla felt something inside of her light up as he approached.

People stepped aside as he approached her at the bar. His presence was enough for any species to take notice of him and to make way. He had a darkness about him that was sexy and a turn-on even Isla couldn't ignore.

"Interesting choice of venue, tonight."

He was so close she could feel the energy pulsating from him. Looking over at Selene, who was now flirting with an Otherworlder, she said, "I had little choice in the matter." A small smile told her he was well aware of his sister's persuasiveness.

He was much different at work. In control. Even though he was here with her, she caught his occasional glances scanning the room keeping tabs on everything in a subtle way. "And she got you to have a few drinks I see."

She had left her sense of self-righteousness at the door. Seeing her relaxed rather than on edge was refreshing. The Wolf in him pushed him to get closer to her. Leaning against the bar, he gave in. Her face was slightly flushed from the alcohol. She didn't need to wear make-up, she was sexy as she was. Her scent danced through the air, teasing him. He wondered if she tasted as good as she smelled. Thinking about tasting her made him a little hard. Shifting, he tried to keep himself in check. He hadn't even touched her yet tonight and he was already wanting to take her back to his office to explore all of her. "I believe you said, and I quote, 'It dulls the senses.'"

When he teased her, she got flushed even more. The pull of her scent drew Axel in closer to her, as he took a deep, intoxicating breath of her.

Isla's heart began to race with excitement as he drew closer. "How do you say no to Selene?"

Isla briefly looked up past Axel. Then, seeing Cami staring at them, she pulled back from Axel altogether. "Plus, I'm not the one working and getting felt up by my help." Axel cocked an eyebrow at the undertone in her statement. Jealousy was not a characteristic he would associate with her. Not at all, in fact. However, it was turning him on. As much as he should have been taken aback by her comment, he wasn't. He liked that she was a little jealous.

Closing the space between them, he leaned in closer to her. She felt a flutter in her stomach which she immediately pushed away, trying desperately to stay in control. As Axel brought his nose to her neck Isla's body responded to him, wanting him to touch her. He nuzzled her neck ever so slightly, feeling the sizzle ignite when their skins touched.

He kissed her lower neck, noticing the softness of her skin. His lips warmed her with each kiss. Then, he moved his mouth to her ear. "Are you jealous, princess?"

His tone of intrigue was irritating but the feeling of him washed over her. Her pulse kicked up a notch as she felt his warm breath on her. The air between them crackled for a moment. She felt a need to be in his arms. His dark brown eyes were captivating. Holding her breath for a second, she grounded herself using the bar for support. She waited to see if he would take one more step to close the little space that was between them to kiss her. Anticipation made her heart race.

She glanced up at the VIP area to see that Cami was still watching them. If looks could kill, she would be shooting lasers with her eyes to turn her to ash on the spot. Isla took a deep breath to push the burning need to touch him away, taking control of herself. When she found her voice, she said, "I'm not the jealous one. How long have you been fucking her for?"

Her question made Axel pause, taking a small step back. Axel noticed how out of place Cami looked staring at them instead of attending to the VIP guests. One look from Axel and Cami turned away and walked out of view. "It was nothing serious. Just an occasional hook-up. She knows that."

"From the looks of it, I don't think she is on the same page as you."

Axel shook his head, "She's been told her position. I made clear there was nothing more there than for me to let off steam, and that now it is over. Don't let it bother you. There was never anything there of substance. All of it happened before our announcement." How convenient that their announcement was only a few weeks old.

Part of Isla was relieved to hear it was nothing serious, but another part was taken aback by it. Still, having seen the look on Cami's face there was something more. Even if it was one-sided.

"Look. Things that happened in the past are just that. History. Can't change it. Can't undo it. I didn't think my parents would commit to the arrangement with your pack. I was surprised when my Alpha committed so early on in the courtship. Things are different now." *Things are changing fast.*

"Because of the mating?" He didn't come across as someone who knows much about commitment. Had he even been in a serious relationship before?

"That, among other things." Scanning the VIP area Axel stood up tall. The relaxed, seductive, playful Axel was gone, replaced by the all-business version. "Fuck."

Isla looked around confused. "What is it?"

"Bad news is what. Bad fucking news." Speaking quickly into his com unit, Axel grabbed Isla's arm. "I want you to get Selene and get out of here. Go directly back to the estate. Don't let her stop for *anything*. Anything." His tone cut through the air sending her a warning. Having never seen him this serious, she knew not to question his instructions.

Axel led Isla through the crowd towards Selene, who greeted them with, "Axel, what is going on?"

Looking at Selene, he responded, "You're out." Isla expected Selene to brush him off, back-talk him, or something. But something unsaid was exchanged between them and Selene took Isla, heading back through the crowd.

"Selene, what is going on?" Isla finally asked again

Weaving through the crowd was a task. "Party's over, that's what." A large group of rowdy college patrons crowded the entry, making it impassable. "Come on, we'll go out the side emergency exit."

Without wasting time Selene focused on their new route.

"I thought Axel said to go out the front?"

Keeping a hold of her arm, Selene pushed her way through people. "Yeah, well, what's important is that we get out of here."

CHAPTER 17

Temporary relief washed over them as they reached the side exit. Though initially she welcomed the stale cold night air, the quietness of the alley gave Isla shivers as the door to the club closed behind her. A soft breeze brought the smell of smoke and old tequila. Isla turned her head to the source of the smell, towards the dark shadows in the alleyway. Two Shadow Demons stepped out from the darkness, making themselves visible. "What's the rush, ladies?"

Selene took a step away from them until a third stepped in front of her. "Why are you leaving so soon?" The smell of rotten flesh rolled off of him. Alarms rang in Isla's head. This was bad, she knew that they should have gone out the front.

Isla pulled Selene back behind her as she stepped forward. Sternly she commanded, "Move out of our way."

"Or what?" his breath rotted its way through the air, churning their stomachs. It took everything for Isla to stay in control and focused, not to throw up from the stench. Dark black eyes filled with emptiness stared at her. *I think I will play with you a little before I eat you. You will be begging for me to kill you. His evil smile showed off his rotting teeth.*

Quickly Isla assessed her surroundings. The barely lit alley offered only one way out: through them. The Shadows crept their way closer to them, predators stalking their prey. Isla needed to get them out of here. With the flick of her wrist, she threw her enchanted whip out towards the Shadows, making them jump back. Her attack offered Selene enough room to break away, but she didn't move. To Isla's surprise, Selene moved in on the Shadow with dragon's breath, pulling a blade from her belt.

They were outnumbered. No easy escape route. Isla had to keep on the offense to even things out. She rounded her whip around her and sent it on an attack, slashing the first Shadow. Black blood drew where it ripped the flesh from his body. However, her aim was a little off and she failed at snatching her target by the neck. "Bitch! You'll pay for that."

Anger overtook the Shadow as he lunged for her. His lack of control gave Isla an opening to take a second shot, ripping his head from his body. The second Shadow came flying over the headless body as it fell to the ground. Isla took a defensive stance, bracing for his attack whilst struggling to pull her whip back around in time.

A gunshot echoed from the end of the alley as the Shadow dropped dead mid-air. Axel and one of his pack members closed in on the space with Dragon's breath. Selene took a step back, trying to catch her breath and give Axel a clear shot.

"Hey, hey, hey man." Dragon's breath took a step back, putting his hands up in surrender, "I don't want no problems man."

Axel approached closer, keeping the gun pointed at his target, ready to fire another round. As he closed in on the last Shadow Axel didn't take his eye off the target for even a second. One wrong move and he would meet the same ending as his fellow Shadow Demons. "Tregger, looks to me like you got a big fucking problem trying to pick off people from my club."

He blew out his breath in dismay. "Oh…This is *your* club. Naw' just was checkin' out who was hangin' in the alley. Didn't know these were your regulars. Didn't know at all."

Axel placed the muzzle of his barrel on the side of the Tregger's head. "Now you know. Not in there. Not out here. Not anywhere near my fucking club."

His dragon's breath soured the air. When he closed his mouth, the stench lessened but the smell of rotting flesh still lingered. "Got it. It was a mistake. One that I got the worst of." Glancing down at his two very dead Shadows oozing into black piles of muck, he added, "One that I won't be making again." Briefly, he looked at Isla before focusing back on Axel, who snapped, "Find your meal elsewhere."

Without another word, he started to walk back towards the darkness of the alley. As he snapped his fingers, three more Shadow Demons stepped out of the darkness and followed him.

CHAPTER 18

Once Tregger was out of view Axel lowered his gun but kept it within a firm grip. His blood boiled in anger, and his Wolf stirred inside of him––livid that Isla had been out here with the low-life Demons. Shadows were a nasty kind of demon to tangle with. She had come close to being attacked. Seeing the Shadow within arm's reach, close enough to have attacked her, made his Wolf want to go after Tregger and finish him off. He knew Tregger wouldn't let this go and that worried him.

Axel took a deep breath, trying to calm down. It angered him that Isla had been in a fight that she was not equipped to handle. She underestimated the Shadows who ran in packs. For someone who was a trained warrior, she had made a big mistake not evaluating her surroundings. Clenching his jaw shut he tried to swallow his anger.

Axel watched Trey walk up to Selene as she recapped how they had ended up in the alley. "I didn't get a scent on them until Tregger walked out of the darkness. By then it was too late." Trey was a good listener and would take note of every detail. Axel was relieved she came out unscathed.

As big and tough as Trey was, his attentiveness and tender care for Selene made Isla feel uncomfortable and awkward in front of Axel. She looked down and walked past him to unhook the end of her whip from the headless Shadow.

Had they gone out the front this wouldn't have happened. Running his free hand through his hair Axel loosened up a little and walked over to her. "Are you ok?" His hand rested softly on her shoulder. His touch melted some of the tension away and grounded her after her adrenaline high. But it didn't erase the frustration she felt.

"Fine," she said as she brought her whip to her arm it shaped it back into its bracelet form. This was not the place to talk about all that happened.

Axel was on the verge of breaking into the Underground's big rings. Tregger and his group could not have picked a worse time to make a move on his territory. Getting in with the bosses of the Underground would give him the power he needed. This business move would connect him with the Underground and the many clans that actively ran between the two worlds.

It also wasn't the most ideal time to begin the mating traditions with Isla and for their packs to come together. How she would fit into everything, he still would have to figure out. But he also couldn't have her getting hurt, or worse: getting in the way. "I'm glad you're fine."

He knew she wasn't fine. When he touched her he sensed her stress. The electric connection he felt earlier was gone. Off like a light switch.

The thought of being mated to someone who might never have unconditional love for her saddened Isla. She wasn't sure what she had expected. Their arrangement was business. He was obligated to check up on her. To make sure she was ok. It would be bad for business if something happened to her on his watch, let alone in his territory.

Axel was irritated by Isla giving him the cold shoulder. "It would be best for you ladies to go back to the estate and call it a night. Trey, we have business to wrap up inside." The loss of electricity that had been humming between them earlier in the night made Axel feel numb. His Wolf did not like it and was pouting. Part of Axel wanted to touch her and bring her against him, but he knew he had other priorities. After taking one last look at her, doing a once over to ensure he didn't see any injuries, he walked away.

The shutting of the metal door echoed through the dark, empty, ally. There was nothing there but the cold night's stale air and a puddle of slimy tar of the decayed Demons. "Come on." Selene linked her arm with Isla and pulled her out of the alley.

Stepping into the bustling nightlife of downtown was energizing. People moving about the street, waiting to get into clubs, made the attack seem like a distant memory. Isla looked at Selene who was wearing a smile. "The night is still young." The carefree, bubbly Selene woke up to meet Isla's grin. "Plus, he only said *it would be best*. Sounded like a suggestion to me." Game on.

CHAPTER 19

Trey followed Axel back to his office. Plagued by mixed emotions, Axel paced for a few moments before pouring a drink. Tonight was a setback. Tregger ran with one of Doyle's Demon clans who frequented the human realm. Axel had been working on building a business relationship with Raven to make a connection with Doyle.

He ran a hand through his hair.

First, Raven had shown up in his club with a number of his clan members. It was not safe for Selene and Isla to remain with Raven lurking so near so he had tried to send them away. Raven was dangerous and deadly. If one thing had gone in his favor tonight, the unexpected visit with Raven taught him Doyle's clans had not been behind the breakout from the Underground. News of the Crazed attacking his gathering had spread like wildfire in the Underground. News of Crazed being undetected was the latest gossip.

"Raven, I had never seen Crazed who did not smell of death. Nor ones that waited to attack." Axel paused, letting Raven process the information.

"Maybe your pack has lost their sense of smell?" The jab at his pack missing the scent of a dozen Crazed was insulting, but it would not be worth it to show his emotions.

Raven had no reason to trust him. He was a Werewolf who lived in the human realm and had no reputation in the Underground. "Let's say three dozen highly skilled warriors who have experience tracking and killing Crazed all missed the Crazed scent. Let's say some of the elders who have been around for one hundred years had not picked up their scent. How* *do you explain that the Crazed maintained control, waited to kill... kept themselves from being seen in plain sight, at the party? It wasn't as if they jumped out of the shadows and engaged in a surprise attack. They were mixed in with the crowd, blending in, perfectly. Waiting."*

Axel knew he'd hit home when Raven didn't have a reply as he sat back in his chair. "Whoever is supporting Erik the Red has started a dangerous war. There is now an enemy no one has ever seen before."

Raven spoke up, "If everything you said is true, this is concerning. I can assure you Doyle and those that follow him would not be behind this." As much as each race thought they were superior to the next, there was a balance between the Underground and the human realm. If one was overtaken and the realms became unbalanced, the survival of all species would be threatened. *"Axel, I will get back to you. Doyle will be most interested in this information."*

After Raven and his crew left, Trey had alerted him there was trouble in the alley. The security screen showed Tregger and his shadows closing in on Selene and Isla. Ice had run through his veins as he darted out of his office to the alley.

CHAPTER 20

As they drove up to the estate, Isla was beyond appreciative that Selene had a driver. Alcohol had washed away the tension from earlier. Still, she wasn't ready to walk through the doors back into her reality. After saying goodnight to Selene, Isla walked around to the back of the grounds. The calm of the night was peaceful. Looking down towards the lake she got lost in the quiet of the moment.

The faint smell of sweet smoke and bourbon danced through the night's air. She didn't need to turn around to know who was behind her. A small feeling of guilt washed over her. She had not come back to the estate after the conflict in the alley like he had instructed her to do. Unexpectedly, Axel walked down to her and stood next to her for a moment as he took in the same view. The silence was deafening but she refused to be the first one to break it.

"Walk with me." The gentleness of his voice invited her to follow him and they walked for some time in silence towards the lake. The large mansion slowly shrank in the background. "I come out here often to think and get away from things. Sort things out. No interruptions."

The lake drew them closer as they walked, welcoming them. Moonlight danced across the glassy water pulling them closer like moths to a flame. "This property, the entire territory for that matter, has been in my family for generations."

Legend had it that the lake had special healing powers. When the Shadow Pack won the battle for this territory, the Lady of the Lake had blessed the Griffith family and had entrusted them to be her keepers.

She acted as a source of power during battle, using the moonlight as a gift. Since the battle of the lands--which had been over a century prior—no one had seen Lady of the Lake. Elders told tales of the lake's power that used to glisten at night, full of energy and life. Axel had never seen the light his grandfather had spoken of.

As a kid, Axel would run out to the lake to get away from everything. His grandfather had a heavy hand when teaching him discipline and to toughen up to prepare for battle. He could remember sitting at the lake and hearing singing as the wind danced across the water.

Now he found himself standing next to Isla, who he was expected to mate by the next wolf moon. Axel had never been in a serious relationship before. Otherworlders and humans threw themselves at him and he had never felt the desire to have someone as his permanent companion. To care about someone else, other than caring to satisfy his lusty needs, was entirely foreign to him. When his father told him, he was considering merging their pack with the Midnight Pack, he'd brushed it off. The Shadow Pack had grown successfully on its own and thus he did not see the need. Hell, he did not think Garrett was serious when he agreed to go through with it. And yet here he was, one week's time would start the courtship process and continue the long-standing pack traditions. Oddly enough, things seemed to make sense in a way he did not yet fully understand.

Moonlight kissed Isla's soft skin, highlighting her beauty. When he stepped closer behind her, he could feel the light strum of electricity that connected them. The same electricity that had flowed between them earlier in the night at the club; one he had never felt before with anyone else. The small doses were a tease to what was manifesting between them. Like a drug, he craved to feel more of it each time.

It almost caused him to forget about the war that was coming, about his work trying to get his foot in the door with the bosses of several rings of Otherworlders, and putting his complex relationship with The

Legion aside. The electric tension was an escape from all he was dealing with. He wanted more of her. There was a need growing inside of him that he wasn't used to feeling. His Wolf liked being near her. She calmed him.

Earlier, when she was distant and closed off from him in the alley, he'd noticed this feeling of serenity was gone. He hadn't known what to do, what to say. His mind seized up confused and desperate to find what was no longer there. He froze and did nothing. His muscles had ached in regret. His sex had ached to be inside her.

Closing the small space between them, his body's heat wrapped around her like a blanket. It was comforting. He was not willing to lose what he was feeling.

Feeling him wrap his arms around her, she closed her eyes, wondering why he hadn't done this in the alley when she had needed it. When she had needed him. But he was here now...

Axel continued to keep his arms wrapped around her as they both stared at the lake. She didn't push him away, but she didn't melt into him either. "When I saw you in the alley with the Demons, I honestly didn't know what I felt beside the need to be near you. One minute you were kicking ass... the next, things changed in a blink of an eye, and..." Thoughts of the attack in the alley stirred up something inside of him, a want to protect her. Kissing the top of her head, he tightened his arms around her, securing her protectively against his body. "...if I hadn't come out when I did to neutralize the threat... if Trey and I hadn't come out when we did... I don't want to think about what would have happened." Shaking his head, he pushed the thoughts aside. There was no way they would have made it out of the alley untouched. The Shadows who had been hiding were ready to attack.

She could feel the honesty in his words. "I was handling the situation." She was at a loss what to say to him. When she couldn't recoil the whip fast enough and free it from the first Shadow, she knew she was in trouble but she would have figured it out. She always did.

He smiled. He knew she was tough, but it was a 'what if' he did not want to play out. "I have no doubt that you can handle many situations. Still, something came over me when I saw him lunge for you..." Slowly he ran his fingers down her arm. Electric tension teased him as he lightly brushed her skin, trying to wrap around him like a vine.

The tingle of his touch soothed her. She wanted more. The want made her a little nervous. A knot of anticipation coiled up in her core. She didn't know if it was the Lady of the Lake casting a spell on her, the alcohol numbing her mind, or a little bit of both. Instinctively she pivoted around in his arms. Their bodies stayed seamlessly connected. The electrical charge swirled around them, keeping them pressed against each other.

No one had ever looked at her or touched her the way Axel was doing right now. Growing up, every sexual relationship she had was no strings attached. She never allowed herself to get emotionally attached to anyone. She never wanted them to feel she wanted more than just sex. She was the granddaughter of the pack leader after all--trained to focus on her duty to one day become the keeper of The Realm, to lead the pack. Males were afraid to get close to her. To cross the pack leader would mean death. Sure, she had explored things from time to time, but never had anyone captivated her the way Axel was doing. Never had she felt whatever it was she was feeling.

Deep down, she knew she wanted desperately to find someone to fall in love with. She had hoped that one day she and Axel would find love, even if it were in her dreams. But right here, right now, everything felt right between them. Chasing a dream that may never come true. Strange how a selfish desire was wickedly seductive.

As she looked up at him, he was bewitched by her. Slowly he leaned down, kissing her gently. Testing her. When she welcomed his kiss, he wanted more of her. Kisses deepened when desire took control, driving him to claim her mouth. The taste of her was like a fine bourbon, smooth on the tongue with a sweet taste. Raw desire pulsed through him. He lost himself, needing all of her. *Mine.*

When she finally broke their kiss, she was caught in a dreamy state, trying to catch her breath. He continued to trail his kisses down her neck. Her taste and smell were intoxicating. The trail of kisses led down to her exposed shoulder. A faint smell of blood from the fight still lingered on her.

She was too perfect to be stained with death, no matter how lightly. "Come." Gently he pulled her into the lake, undressing her piece by piece as they walked deeper into the water. As cool as the night was, the lake was warm and inviting. Faint flutters of light glistened around their bodies, coming to life as they moved deeper into the lake.

He needed her as much as she wanted him right now. Her pulse was racing with desire. Her core tightened in excitement. "Axel...I..." she stumbled to find words. When he heard his name whispered through her soft delicate lips he couldn't help but kiss her again, devouring her before she could speak another word.

He wrapped his arms around her and lifted her up. Isla wrapped her legs around his waist, welcoming him into her sex. She gasped. He felt so good. He felt right. Everything inside of her melted.

They moved in a rhythm of passion which slowly built up until they both needed more and couldn't stop.

The faint glow in the water around them slowly regained its light, illuminating brighter as they continued to chase their climax. The more she squeezed his sex, riding him, taking control, the harder it was for him to keep hold of his self-discipline.

Axel pulled back from kissing her, breathing rapidly. The sound of her taking short deep breaths was so sexy. Keeping hold of her, he slid one hand down to the core of her pleasure, providing extra friction and sending her sex into overdrive. He exploded as she hit her orgasm.

"Ah, Axel!" He captured her mouth with his as he wanted the moment all to himself. He would make her scream his name again before the night ended.

His finger continued to massage her, guiding her to ride him. Her hips moved in response to his command as she shivered and her body lost control orgasming again at the sensation. He rode the second wave, pumping his seed inside of her. *Mine.* The need to mark her was tempting. There would be no stopping it if he let his beast out now. No going back. Hovering over her neck he could just bite her and form their blood bond. He wasn't sure if he could just stop there. Finding a sliver of control, he pulled back from the temptation that pulled his every desire.

Isla rested her head on his shoulder, and they stood in the comfort of the lake, still bound together. Neither one wanted to break away. The lake's water sparkled around them, full of life.

After a few minutes, she found her breath and grounded herself. Isla unwrapped her legs from his waist. He still held onto her as they walked closer to the shoreline.

Dusk was starting to wake on the horizon. Light shimmered, breaking through the darkness. Axel kissed her softly as the burn to take her again surged through him. From now on, he would be keeping her all to himself.

CHAPTER 21

Sex lasted until the early hours of the morning. Afterward, Axel stayed to watch Isla sleep for a while. He never imagined he would feel such a connection with her. It was a pleasant surprise, but this was the worst time to be distracted. With a sigh, he got up and left her room. With Otherworlders making alliances and a war brewing, he needed to stay focused. He had been selfish last night when he gave in to his desire, and it was something he could not let happen again.

The Legion was anxious to make a move against Erik the Red, the powerful Crazed Vampire who had escaped the Underground, as rumors surfaced he was building his own army of Crazed. An offensive advantage was a necessary play to try to stop the war before it started. The Legion, led by a Vampire who was long rumored to be the rightful king to lead his kind in the Underworld, fought for balance between both worlds.

Axel racked his brain about how he could keep Isla out of the war. In the end, there was no solution. She was in it whether he liked it or not. The sooner he embraced it, the sooner he could figure out how to keep her at a distance the best he could. If he brought her into his world, he could keep a close eye on her. He struggled with his decision throughout the day as he weighed his options. In the end, he knew there was no other way.

She didn't ask any questions when he asked her to go with him tonight for business. The drive into the city was quiet. She had a lot of questions, but she wasn't sure where to start. "How much of this does your pack know?"

As he kept his eyes on the road, with only short breaks in contact when he checked the route to his rendezvous point with The Legion, he said, "As much as I tell them. Which is little. Mostly, they know I run a lucrative business. Meanwhile, I am making calculated and purposeful connections. My business moves have been profitable, so no one complains as long as the money continues to be plentiful." That was especially true for his Alpha. Greed would be Garrett's downfall.

That's what was so surprising about his Alpha had made the commitment to the arranged mating with Isla. What value he saw was unclear. Her pack did not have the financial resources as the Shadow Pack did. Checking the navigation once again, Axel put the thoughts out of his mind. He would find out his Alpha's motivation sooner or later.

The chemistry between them was positive, strong, and so he wasn't complaining. He could see spending his life with her after things settled. She would make a great partner. She could handle herself and wasn't afraid to get her hands dirty. Much unlike the other females he had had around for entertainment in the past. No, she could handle herself with her whip and take care of business and she was dead sexy while doing it. Thinking back to the night of the gathering, when he watched her wield the whip, made his sex throb.

However, none of this was any reason for Garrett's commitment to their union. If there was one thing he knew about his father, it was that he was always motivated by greed. Sure, Isla had protected his mom, who Garrett loved, but that could have been repaid with a simple thank you and a few invitations to coming gatherings. But Axel knew that sooner or later Garrett would tip his hand... And when he did, he would need to be prepared.

He pulled into the parking garage and parked alongside two black SUVs. "The Legion has a bad reputation for being trigger happy and old school. We both want to stop the war before it starts." She nodded. Keeping her eyes on the blacked-out SUVs, she followed Axel's lead getting out and standing in front of his Land Rover.

The doors of both SUVs opened and large male Vampires of The Legion exited. To Axel, it was clear that they did not remotely attempt to hide they were packing heat.

Jax stepped in front of the rest of the group. "Didn't know it was 'bring a date to the meeting' night. Hello sweetheart."

Axel had never had issues with any member of The Legion, but Jax might become the first. The beast inside him was on guard and did not like Jax's attempt to flirt with Isla. She was his. Taking a protective step toward her he said, "Didn't know I needed such a welcoming committee to meet with Griffin." Jax listened to Axel but kept his eyes on Isla. She stared right back at him. Motionless. Unimpressed.

"Business is business." He gave her another look over and noted the enchanted whip wrapped around her wrist as a decorative bracelet. "Fine, armed, and I hear dangerous. Not bad for daddy telling you to get hitched. We said to come alone and you come with a plus one. We said come unarmed and your plus one is *armed*. She needs to get rid of it before Griffin arrives." A moment of silence stretched between them as Isla narrowed her eyes at Jax. There was no way she'd be taking off her whip, unless she was unsheathing it to teach him a lesson.

Jax responded to her snarl with a smile, exposing the tips of his fangs. "But for real. Damn, Axel, didn't know times were changin' so much you got a female acting as your backup. Darlin', you get tired of him, give me a call. I'll make it worth your time." Jax winked at her.

Before Axel could step in front of Isla to cut him off, Isla coolly side-stepped him. "Go ahead and try to take it from me. It might be the last thing you touch with your pretty little hands."

Smiling, he stepped forward, ready to accept the challenge. *You will be the next thing my pretty little hands touch. I'll show you what you're missing, being with a dog.* The other warriors started chattering, taking bets on how fast Isla could take him down with her whip. Lowell threw down his smoke as his voice cut through the bullshit in the air. "Enough. The female can come with us."

Jax shot a glance at Lowell, who nodded at the garage entrance. "We don't have time for games. Get ready to roll."

A third blacked-out SUV drove up with the passenger-side window rolled down. "Get in," a deep voice commanded. Isla fell in line with Axel. He opened the door and quickly assessed the SUV, surprised to see that Griffin had Marcus seated next to him. He motioned for Isla to get in first before following her inside.

It was hard for Isla to read anyone's thoughts, which frustrated her. It was like everyone was on a different radio frequency that she couldn't tune into unless they were tuned into her. Fucking vampires.

CHAPTER 22

Once they reached their destination, they filed out into a massive underground garage filled with SUVs and sports cars. Overhead fluorescent lights illuminated the garage. Isla kept her hand on her wrist as she followed Axel into the building.

"You can relax. No one will make a move without my command," Griffin said as he nodded at the light hold she had on her wrist, ready to fire away if need be. He sat down at the head of the table. "Axel, you know, you are a hard guy to get a hold of."

"Circumstances haven't been favorable recently." The warriors agreed. A few weeks ago, Lincoln had brought Erik the Red into Axel's club. Even though they had had Erik the Red within reach, they had lost their window to take him out. The Legion had been on the hunt for a second round with him, one that would take him and his gang of Crazed bastards out.

It was no secret the courtship party had been infiltrated by Crazed who went undetected, but how was still the question they needed answers to. Axel gave everyone the same debrief he had given Raven the other night. The Crazed entered unnoticed, with no stench. Their most trained Wolves didn't detect them.

"Still this doesn't answer how they've masked their scent. How they stayed in control and did not go on a killing rampage until the very end." The growing development was a problem. For Erik the Red to have a gang of trained Crazed was unheard of. No one ever thought it was possible. They were missing something.

Bo looked around and asked, "What was the point of crashing your party anyways if they weren't there to make you all their meal?"

"Hard to say. Isla thinks that they were testing us." The group broke out in a chatter of disbelief that the Crazed had enough control to have calculated actions.

Griffin stopped the arguing by slamming his fist down on the table. He looked at Isla who was standing tall and motionlessly. "Why do you think that?"

"Ah come on Griff, what could she possibly know about all this?" Jax couldn't help but take another jab at her.

He clearly started to wear thin on Axel's patience so Isla stepped in before Axel could say or do something he couldn't take back. "Just like you have been trying to push his buttons for a reaction, I think they were testing out their offensive tactics. The Crazed must have had a man on the inside to get through the basic security checkpoint, but whatever has allowed them to evolve so they could mask their odor and go inside completely undetected was pretty new."

The group processed the undertaking to get to someone on the inside as a regular Otherworlder. Add being Crazed and having to mask death's odor, plus the constant need to feed off the living, and it was easy to see that just entering took planning and preparation on a new level. No one had any doubt Erik the Red was involved in orchestrating the plan in the background. The question was, with who? Or who did he get to?

"What else are you thinking? You're holding something back." Griffin could smell it in the air.

Isla had her own personal theory, one that she hadn't shared with Axel, her Alpha, or the pack during the debrief. Something kept bothering her about the attack and the response from the Shadow Pack that night.

She looked up at Axel, waiting for his nod for her to share. He didn't like not knowing what she was going to say. Even more so, it was something she hadn't shared with him and that he needed to talk to her later about later.

Taking a deep breath, she looked around the room. The Legion waited for her response. "When the attack was underway and the Shadow Pack was fighting back, no one changed into hybrid Were-form." Axel thought back through the events of that night and realized she was right. Not that they needed to change, the threat was taken out swiftly. But thinking back, it was odd that when Lilly was in trouble, Garrett never changed. The life of a mate being threatened would drive any bonded male into overdrive with the need to protect her at all costs, including changing into his deadliest form.

Axel asked the question many of them were thinking, "Do you think Garrett was behind the setup?" It pained him to even suggest it. Garrett was his father and his Alpha.

It was a question Isla had thought about a lot as she replayed the events over and over to try to understand how everything could have even happened. "At first I wondered about that. He wanted to protect Lilly when he saw she was in trouble but didn't shift. But not a single other Werewolf shifted into their hybrid form or Wolf form that night." Not being able to change would scare any Werewolf. One would be shamed and cast out of the pack if he could no longer shift. A whole pack not able to change? That was a taboo topic.

"I think there were multiple objectives that night. One we already identified, the Crazed getting in undetected. The second, a recon mission to test out their offensive advantage."

"One that failed." Many of the warriors agreed with Bo.

Isla brought the room back by cutting through the chatter, "It depends on how you look at it. If it was a suicide mission to begin with, to gather intel, then it wasn't a failure. If another objective was to test out the pack's response and my defensive ability... success. If something was done to prevent the pack from being able to transition and they do not even realize it, the mission was a victory."

That was a lot of "ifs". No one brushed off her wonderings. Hell, it made them all take a step back and rethink what they were really dealing with.

"Bad day to be a Werewolf, I guess," Jax muttered. Not being able to transition into your true state of being when you are at your most powerful was not something anyone wanted to think about.

Griffin was the first to break the heavy silence. "Bad day for all of us if what they used could affect any Otherworlder's ability undetected. A magical sedative to lessen the opponent's ability to attack, is a weapon of mass destruction. Let's hope she's wrong, or that we can strike before they figure out how to use whatever it is on a larger scale. If she's right, they are going to test their weapon again."

Erik the Red needed to be taken out. Whoever was helping him would meet a death sentence. They all agreed on that. There was no way his breakout from the Underground, alongside twelve other dangerous, Crazed Otheworlders, had happened on its own. He had been locked away for centuries with no contact with the outside world, and within a few months, he was already forming an army and possessed a weapon no one had ever seen or heard of...which was certainly not a coincidence.

Everything had gone off the rails after The Legion's encounter with Lincoln and his organization a few months back. "Stirring up shit with Tregger didn't help." Regardless of the situation, Tregger was another setback. "He was a good lead, maybe our only lead to get a beat on Erik the Red." Griffin's thoughts were second by his team.

It was easy for them to criticize when they were not the ones with people on the line. "Look. It's not ideal, I agree. At the end of the day, he stepped out of line waiting in the shadows around my club. Let alone trying to go after Selene and Isla. He started it and I finished it. I didn't touch Tregger, just his Shadows."

A few less Shadow Demons lurking around on the streets wasn't anything anyone was shedding a tear over. Pissing off Tregger was another story. Losing the connection with Tregger? A lost opportunity in more ways than one. But that was Axel's problem to deal with, not The Legion. Axel may be a valuable ally to The Legion, but he was not part of their brotherhood.

Not much was said on the drive back to the garage after the meeting. Isla tried reading Axel's thoughts but he was closed off. Normally Isla tried to push out everyone's thoughts and control her gift. Finding herself on the other side, not being able to easily tap into people's thoughts, was frustrating. She didn't know what was going on with her; everything had felt upside down since she'd found out about having to go through with the mating.

After The Legion left the garage, Axel kept his distance. Was he upset? Did she say something that offended him? She watched him, lost as he was in his own thoughts.

"Drive back to the estate without me. I got business to take care of." He handed her the keys without waiting for a response. More interested in his phone than her. Just like that. Last night didn't seem to have happened.

Axel watched Isla drive off before making the call. "Trey give me the coordinates."

CHAPTER 23

As she watched Winston leave to deal with pack-related business, Isla pondered how things were getting increasingly confusing. Axel hadn't come in last night from whatever "business" he had to attend to. She wondered if Axel was avoiding her intentionally, regretting getting too involved with her. It wouldn't be the first time she had dealt with something like it.

She wondered if this was what her life was going to be like? Axel out whenever and wherever he wanted to while she was stuck at the estate waiting around for him? Everything was so complicated. For once, she just wanted things to be easy. Thoughts of Cami staring her down in the club rushed back to her. Did he go back to his club to be with her? Was that his "business"? Jealousy boiled up in Isla. She walked out of her room as she let her mind wander.

She was thankful to find the training room abandoned. As she worked out, she tried to process everything between her and Axel. They were set to be mated. There had been a few moments of connecting and exploring their chemistry. Chemistry was not an issue. Axel seemed to care for her. But then again, maybe he was caring out of obligation. Did the courtship mean they were in a relationship? So many questions. No answers. Just when she thought things were progressing, the emergency brake was put on, everything coming to a stop.

"I think you have beaten the dummy to its last leg." She took a step back from the target, startled by Duke's voice. "You seem to have something on your mind."

Duke made her feel uncomfortable and out of place. She walked over to the weapons rack trying to focus on something, anything but him. He was the last person she wanted to talk to.

"It's nothing."

His humph of disagreement floated towards her. "Would that nothing be about Axel not coming home last night?" *No doubt wrapped up with one of those fine workers of his who knew how to get a man off. Axel knows how to hire the ladies.*

Whilst forcing her mind to shut out his thoughts, she avoided looking at him. There was no point in trying to say anything. Not that she had to explain herself to Duke, of all people.

"Things are complicated, which is to be expected seeing as we are just getting to know each other."

Duke gently brushed up against Isla as he joined her at the weapons rack. The touch made her feel uncomfortable and tense. Taking a small step to the side she put a little space between them so that he wasn't touching her. As he inspected a few of the weapons he continued, "Not sure how complicated things can be when two people are open and honest with each other. Secrets, on the other hand... Secrets make things really complicated. Wouldn't you agree?"

She wasn't sure where he was going with this, but if agreeing with him would shut him up, so be it. "I suppose you're right." A small, nervous knot was forming in her stomach. She personally did not care for Duke, especially after the night of the attack in the debriefing room he had made it clear her thoughts were not valued. He was Garrett's second in command and a well-respected leader in the pack. She was not valued.

He stopped meddling with the weapons, turning to her, as he closed the little space that was left between them. She froze, holding her breath. "Relationships are complicated like a weapon." Duke slowly traced the whip that rested peacefully on her wrist. His finger trailed off the whip periodically and touched her skin, sending shivers where their bodies touched. Her arm felt heavy as she slowly pulled it away. "Not like the whip you have grown so accustomed to. No, like a new weapon ready to be learned. Ready to be handled. You have to start slowly to get to know it. Work it too fast, you might get hurt." His words sent a shiver down her spine. Trying to force herself to breathe slowly and stay calm was a struggle when her ears started to ring with a warning. "Here." Handing her a set of silver daggers, he continued, "Let's work with these. They are a great tactical weapon."

In one split second, his tone changed from a low, dark, unsettling tone, to all business. Duke focused on the training targets, giving her instructions on how to handle the hilt of the dagger.

Engaging in Dagger Lesson 101 sent Isla's mind into overdrive. Breaking out of her shocked state Isla slowly followed him to the throwing area keeping a tight grip on the daggers. The small knot in her stomach lessened, but it was still there. She didn't trust him. Not one bit.

Confused and blindsided by what had just happened, her head was spinning, trying to sort everything out. *Get it together.* She had to be losing her mind. She didn't know why she stayed when everything in her was telling her to run. Maybe to prove something to herself, like that she was overreacting?

The first few throws landed everywhere but where they were supposed to. Even with Duke's explicit instructions, she couldn't focus on the target, the blades flying past it. One blade hit the target, though the hilt of the dagger bounced off and lightly ricocheted the blade back towards her. She sucked at this.

Unable to hide her frustration, Isla let out a loud sigh. Duke went down to the target and picked up the one lonely blade that lay on the ground with the rest of the blades sticking in the wall.

"Ok. Let's try something else. Close your eyes."

What was the point? She clearly didn't have a talent for wielding daggers. But she listened to Duke and closed her eyes. She could hear his footsteps stop behind her. The knot in her stomach grew tighter as his hand brushed her arm, placing the dagger in her throwing hand as he stood behind her.

Stop it. He's just trying to teach you something. Her body was uncomfortable with how close he was, tensing up, becoming rigid.

"Think of this as your last dagger in a fight you are not winning. Your opponent is advancing on you." His hands firmly grasped her hips as he pivoted her body into a defensive stance. His touch felt wrong. Holding her breath, she tried measuring the placement of his hands on her body with the depth of his touch. Was he making a move on her or just giving a seriously inappropriate lesson? The more she thought about it, the more time he had to continue his lesson. The more his hands were on her body. Gripping the dagger tighter in her hand, palm sweaty, she felt anything but empowered. She felt trapped and unsure of what to do. Her heart pounded in her chest.

He slid his hands down her side as he stepped closer to her, guiding her hips to move into a throwing stance. "Grasp the blade in your throwing hand like it is your last hope. Feel the slight curves of the blade." His body briefly brushed against her backside. A lump formed in her throat and she swallowed hard.

"Now ease up on the grip just slightly." Moving his hand to her right arm, he guided her arm up into a throwing stance. His body pressed up against hers, paralyzing her. He leaned down to her ear. His warm breath made every hair on the back of her neck stand up. Her chest tightened as panic built. Silence stretched between them, though she could hear her heart beating in her ears. "When I give the command, open your eyes and throw your dagger at the target without hesitation." After another brief moment of silence, he bellowed, "Now!" The change in his tone and the directness startled her, but she did as he said and threw the dagger at the target. After soaring through the air, the blade hit the target in the chest.

"Not bad." Taking a step away from her, Duke watched Isla's

every move. "Next time we will have to perfect your aim. Each throw to the heart. Kill shots. And increase your success ratio. This was what... one out of twenty throws? You can do better."

Throwing the blade had gotten her out of her state of paralysis. "Thank you," was all she could muster before she turned and walked out.

CHAPTER 24

Trey gave Axel coordinates to his team's location in an abandoned area outside of downtown. It was an old warehouse in the housing district, alongside homes that were run-down, with bars covering the windows. Some doors were boarded up with spray paint that read, KEEP OUT. No lights lined the streets. Complete darkness. When Axel made the team stop in front of an old warehouse, someone asked, "Are you sure this is the place?"

Nodding, Axel focused on surveying the area. Something didn't add up. The attack at his gathering had been well thought out. Orchestrated. Crazed dressed the part went undetected. As he looked around this dump of an area, Axel thought there was no way whoever was behind the attack would be laying low in such a place. The Crazed may have been able to hide the smell of death, but there was no way they could hide the natural smell this place was giving off.

"Where's Duke's team?" Duke was never late, yet today he was nowhere in sight.

Trey looked at his phone, "They were held up but are en route. Do you want to wait for them?"

Axel sighed. He had a bad feeling about this, but he could not leave until he investigated the lead. At the same time, if this was a dead lead, he would rather clear the building with his most trusted group than waste the time of his pack warriors. Perhaps he and his team could do a quick sweep of the building, and check out if their lead was viable or not. If the lead was dead, he would save Duke and his team time.

Plus, he liked the idea of not having to deal with his father's second in command. The way Duke acted the other night during the debrief still did not sit well with him.

There was no easy way into the building. All of the windows in the front had bars around them and were boarded up. They would be going in blind. Walking to the back, Axel looked for another entry point. There was one door. The windows in the back were not boarded up.

Using his Werewolf senses Axel listened for the smallest noise coming out of place. Nothing. Peering into the window, he could make out no movement. It was hard to see through the thick layer of grime on the window. When he motioned for his team to move in, Hunter opened the door as they filed in one-by-one fanning out into the open space. The smell of decaying bodies was overpowering as soon as they entered. Blood stained the walls and floor, but Axel could not see anything rotting.

Moving through the first floor, they saw rooms filled with dirt, dust, and blood. Whoever was living here did not clean up after themselves. Except for the bodies, apparently.

The pack members kept their guns drawn, ready to fire as they continued to clear rooms. The wood beneath their feet squeaked as they walked through the building. The stench of rotting bodies grew stronger the deeper they moved into the warehouse.

Hunter took a step into the next room, motioning for the team to follow. As he stepped farther into the room, the wood beneath his boots snapped as the flooring broke apart, caving inward, taking Hunter and Koda into the darkness. Trey instinctively pulled Axel back as the floor swallowed his team members.

"Hunter! Koda!" Axel used his flashlight to look for them in the thick cloud of dust.

Sounds of screeching erupted from below. The smell of death hit Axel's nose in warning. "Crazed! Go! Go! Go!" The rest of his team jumped down into the rubble, blinded by a grey cloud of dust, as they opened fire on a swarm of Crazed. Axel and Trey guarded Hunter and Koda as they rose up from under the pile of broken flooring.

It was only a few seconds until the team's gunfire died down. The dead Crazed at their feet started turning to dust. Axel was about to let go of his indrawn breath when debris started falling from the ceiling above them, causing them to look up. Crazed Vampires with bright red eyes lined the ceiling. "Above!" Axel shouted alerting his team.

Hordes of Crazed Vampires dropped from the ceiling to attack them. They had walked into a den of Crazed Otherworlders! Hunter and Koda shifted into their werewolf forms as they charged at the Crazed. One by one, Axel's entire team shifted into their werewolf form, letting their beasts out.

More Crazed Vampires scaled the ceiling towards them as Crazed Wolves charged in from a hallway. A Vampire sliced Axel's arm with his razor-sharp nails, trying to grab at him. Axel's beast roared in anger and dove to rip the throat out of a Crazed.

More howling brought Axel's head around at three Crazed who jumped on top of Koda. Axel leaped over a pile of dead bodies pulling the Crazed off of him, ripping open their necks one by one.

He helped Koda up and pulled him behind him as more Crazed swarmed in from the hallway.

Another Crazed dropped from the ceiling and started tearing at Axel's arm, as two more Crazed jumped on him from the side. Koda and Axel continued to attack. The ripping of his skin sent waves of pain down his arm, angering his beast more. Axel continued fighting with force, each strike a kill shot. Crazed continued to file in from a dark hallway.

The sounds of footsteps brought Axel's attention to the opening above his head. Duke and his backup arrived, jumping down to join the fight. Better late than never.

With the help of Duke's team, the fight was over quickly. The influx of Crazed slowed until there were no more left. The warriors stood on the basement floor drenched in blood. Duke commanded his team, "Clear the hallway. The rest of you, back to the estate. We'll burn this place down. One less den, one less problem."

Axel and his team shifted back to their human states. He agreed with Duke that his team needed to be taken back to the infirmary to be tended to. Their bodies normally healed quickly, but their wounds needed cleaning, to ensure there was no infection from the diseased Crazed. Axel looked at Duke and nodded, thanking him.

CHAPTER 25

Thoughts were racing through her head a mile a minute. The more she tried to make sense of what had just happened, the more she found herself running. Running to put distance between her and the training room. Running to get away from Duke. She didn't know where she was going. Tears flew into the air as she went into the forest trying to outrun her tension.

Finally, her legs gave out and she collapsed next to a large tree, deep into the forest. Tears had stopped pouring down at some point during the run. She had no energy to get up. No energy to cry.

She was mad at herself. Questioning everything that happened today in the training room, everything since she had arrived at the estate. Her world was spiraling out of control and would not stop.

Her mind was spinning. Did Duke make a move on her? Her mind was convinced, but on the other hand, he had kept everything about training. And it had worked in the end.

She didn't like him, that was for sure. Was she over-analyzing everything because Axel was so distant and distracted lately and her Alpha had left her here alone to go back to the pack? Would Duke have been that close to her, touching her the way he did, if Axel was there? If anyone else had been in the room with them? She felt so alone and vulnerable.

Lost in her thoughts, Isla leaned back against a tree. Everything was muddy and confusing. The breeze gently brushed her cheek as she rested her head. Time slowed and a glimmer of sparkling lights surrounded her. Fairies and Sprites came out of hiding.

Finally, she smiled. She loved when they visited. One Sprite danced her way over to her.

Isla it's been too long.

"I agree."

Things have been in constant change. He wants to talk to you.

Isla nodded, then waited patiently and watched as the Fairies and Sprites disappeared back into The Realm when Rattenru appeared life-sized with a pair of warriors standing behind him. Standing up, she greeted Rattenru formally. "Ah child, relax. No need for formalities." Easy for him to say when he comes out guarded by his best fighters.

Rattenru was the leader of Fay in The Realm. Very few knew Isla was his granddaughter. Her Fay blood gave her the unique gift she kept hidden. When her mother had left The Realm and mated with a Werewolf, she was banished. Rattenru forbade her from returning. Afterward, he had only reached out twice to her mom. Once, to bless Isla's birth; and a second time on her birthday when she'd gifted her the enchanted whip.

After Isla's parents were attacked and killed by the Crazed, Rattenru found small pockets of time to visit Isla to give her guidance. She appreciated and valued his visits, but she knew there was great risk each time he did. Risk of him being exposed. Risk of someone finding out Isla's blood connection to Rattenru.

Smiling, she said, "It's good to see you."

"And you as well. I'm afraid I do not have long my dear Isla. The shift in the Underground threatens the safety of The Realm. There are Otherworlders providing aid and pulling the strings of puppets."

Rattenru did not share anything she did not already know. "Will The Realm stand with us when the time comes?"

"The Realm will not be associated with either side. As a keeper of The Realm, you need to eliminate those who threaten it. Be cautious of the ones around you. The Lady of the Lake will help you when the time comes. Trust in her."

Rattenru took a small box from his pocket and handed it to her. "A gift."

Removing the lid of the box revealed a beautiful, translucent, blue, crystal necklace sparkling in the light. When she carefully took it out she noticed the top clasp was a cap to the crystal. "It's beautiful. What is inside it?"

"Wear this to the next gathering. The magical dust is an old Fay healing powder we have used for centuries. A small sprinkle is all that is needed to cure the worst poison."

Rattenru stepped closer to her, placed his hand on her stomach and smiled. "The small life forming inside of you: protect it at all costs. This blessing will bring much joy."

Impossible. There was no way. Panic washed through her. She wasn't even mated. He didn't knot with her, did he? This was the last thing she needed right now. "Isla, I know many things. Do not worry." Giving her a reassuring smile he patted her shoulder.

Sounds of whispers danced through the air. They were too soft for Isla to make out what they were saying. "I must go. You need to return to the estate. Stay strong. Be careful."

Before she could say anything else, Rattenru and his guards had disappeared and the portal to The Realm closed. The light which had surrounded her faded and darkness set in. Looking around the forest, Isla noticed that as the peaceful warmth dissipated, the dark, cold night's air filled the void.

As she walked back up to the estate everything was still. Silence was never a good sign. Light shimmered out of the windows, lighting the path back to the entryway. Stepping inside, she exchanged the quiet of the night for chaos and people running frantically through the hall.

When she reached Selene's side she asked, "What is going on?"

Selene grabbed Islas hand and muttered, "Oh my gosh. Thank the Goddess. You need to come with me. There was an attack. Axel was brought into the infirmary. I barely saw him, but I don't think it is good."

A sick feeling settled in her stomach. Isla found herself jogging to the infirmary. She stopped at the door when she saw Axel sitting up as the doctor finished bandaging his side.

The doctor nodded to Isla as she walked in. "I'll leave you now. You need to rest so you heal properly." Once the door was closed, Isla walked up to Axel to help him put his shirt on. Softly, she traced down the bandage covering his ribs.

"What happened? Are you ok?"

"Aye. I'm ok." He allowed Isla to help him. Once his shirt was on, he sat on the edge of the bed.

She stood in front of him, running her hands through his hair as she gently kissed his forehead. "We had a lead that went wrong. Really wrong. My team was ambushed by a group of Crazed."

"Where were you? How many of them were there?" A million questions were flying through her mind.

Axel took her hands into his and squeezed them. "It was just business. A meeting gone bad." Axel brushed it off as if it was nothing. Isla looked at the bandages under his shirt. This was more serious than just business, as he put it. "Luckily, Duke and his team were close by and were able to respond to our aid. If it wasn't for him, we wouldn't have been able to walk away with only a few scratches."

The mention of Duke's name made bile rise up in her throat. When she swallowed it down, it burned like acid. Looking down into his open shirt, she noticed a small stain of blood starting to seep through the bandage. "This doesn't look like just a scratch..."

Scratch and stabbed, it was the same to Axel. He didn't want to worry her with details. The night was over. He had walked away with injuries that would heal by tomorrow. Pulling his shirt closed he slid off of the bed. Pain shot down his right side making it hard to gain his footing. Isla caught his unbalanced sway placing his arm around her shoulder for support.

"Come on. I need to go to the war room to debrief."

She helped him make his way to the war room, feeling his pain with every step they took. The debrief provided her with a little more information. Axel had thought he was meeting someone with intel on who had helped the Crazed gain access to their gathering. His lead never showed. Instead, his team was ambushed by a large group of Crazed.

"Duke's team saved our ass out there. They were in the right place at the right time." Duke avoided making eye contact with Isla. He accepted the praise with a few quick words about his duty. Isla found it interesting that just a few hours ago he was giving her a lesson with the daggers. Then, he had somehow happened to make it over where Axel was to save the day? How convenient.

"Another targeted attack. I don't like it. The gathering of the packs is nearing, and we are no closer to knowing how the Crazed gained the advantage on us the last time. Axel, you and your team are off rotation for the time being. Any leads need to go to Duke." Garrett paced the room as he continued to bark orders.

CHAPTER 26

As soon as Garrett was done barking marching orders, he ended the meeting. "Axel, I want to talk to you. The rest of you, clear out. You have work to do."

Isla exited the room, following Selene. "Wow. I've not seen Garrett that worried."

"I'm sure tonight's attack involving Axel hit home a little."

Selene stopped before they reached the doors to the patio and waited for Trey to catch up to them.

As they stepped outside, the breeze coming off the lake felt cold and numbing, though the firepit's blaze warmed the air somewhat. Isla listened as Trey filled Selene in on the details of what had happened the night before. Clearly, he trusted his partner with the details, something Axel did not do.

She wasn't sure how long she had been outside before Axel came out and sat beside her. "I figured I might find you out here."

Staring at the moonlight dancing on the top of the lake in the distance she asked, "Why is that?"

"Well, you weren't inside so I figured I would come out here. And you're in good company I see." Selene and Trey looked up and smiled.

The time outside had given Isla time to think without distractions. Looking over, she met his gaze. "I'm glad you and your team are ok."

Axel took her hands into his. He started rubbing them to warm them before bringing her hands to his lips and gently kissing them. "No need to worry. It will take a lot more than a few dozen Crazed to take me out."

Trey laughed along with him and they started talking about a few they had beheaded before backup arrived. Isla forced a smile, she didn't find it amusing even if he was trying to brush it off.

Isla's thoughts drifted to the Gathering of the packs in a few weeks. The breach at the announcement ceremony was still a mystery. And now there had been another attack on the pack, on the alpha's family. First at his own home, threatening the safety of his mate, now one deliberately aimed at Axel. This next Gathering was a big event. Many leaders from the surrounding lands would gather in one place.

"Axel, do you think Garrett wants to postpone the Gathering?"

Axel dismissed the idea with a small grunt dismissed. "He is hell-bent on our mating. He is focused on everything staying on course. Uniting our packs is becoming more important as time passes."

Trey nodded in agreement.

Everything kept leading back to Duke. After tonight's heroic save no one would suspect him of being the rat in the pack. She was sure that Axel wouldn't even entertain the idea. Choosing her words carefully she began, "With a traitor in the pack threatening the security of all operations, what do you think about having Trey take the lead on operations and security for the Gathering?"

Axel looked at her, trying to read her. "Do you think Duke can't handle the operation? He is the second in command and has led the security here for a long time. Not to mention he just saved my tail along with those of several other pack members."

Softening her tone, she said, "With so much going on, with the threat of the Crazed and the possibility that one or more members of the pack could be a traitor, I figured that finding the leak would be a priority for Duke. Trey has proven himself and it's evident you trust him. It might be a relief to Duke to not have one more thing on his plate."

Before Axel could respond, Trey spoke up. "She has a point. It would be doubling our efforts in terms of security."

Trey and Axel had spent the last few days discussing different members of the pack who could be behind the security breach at the announcement ceremony. They primarily looked at those who had been climbing the ranks quickly and those who may think they deserve more than what they have. As large as the Shadow Pack was, everyone needed to be looked at. Right now, they had no leads to go off of.

"With more time on our hands, we could make the security for the next Gathering air-tight. Think about it." Trey gave Selene a look that said it was time to leave the two others alone for the night.

Axel studied Isla as Trey and Selene retired, leaving them alone on the balcony. For a while, the only sound between them was the fire crackling until Axel broke their silence. "Isla what is really on your mind?"

There were a lot of things she wanted to tell him. From what happened in the training room with Duke to what was happening with The Realm. What's more, she considered telling him the truth about her parents and her blood connection to Rattenru. She wondered if he would call everything off if he found out she was not pure-blooded. Would he do that knowing she was pregnant? As she was part Werewolf, her pregnancy would only be a few months and she would start showing soon. She was still processing the news herself. It was simple biology. Werewolves did not get pregnant easily, normally only if they were bonded. Did they bond? Or was she pregnant because she was half Were and half Fay? The questions were spinning through her head.

Whatever she is hiding, I will find out in time.

His thoughts brought her out of her own head. "Axel, do you still want to go through with our mating? Not out of obligation, or because it's what our Alphas want... Do you want it?"

Sighing, Axel said, "Isla what are you thinking about?" *Is this what she is brooding over? Of all things.*

"It's a simple question." Looking down she knotted her hands, fidgeting, waiting for his response. Rattenru was right, she needed to protect the little life that was growing inside her. If Axel didn't want the mating, she would walk away. Him not knowing would be best. She had no idea how she would accomplish that, but she would find a way.

"Why are you questioning the mating?"

She needed to know where he stood. What he wanted. "We met because it's what our pack leaders wanted. *They* want us to be mated. Never asked either of us what we wanted, but my Alpha knew I would fulfill my duty." Isla thought back to how quickly their relationship had developed. They had chemistry. He trusted her, at least she thought he did, since they had their meeting with The Legion. But lately, Axel had been distant. Sometimes they saw each other and spent time together, other times they didn't.

"It's not simple. It's *our* responsibility to our packs to fulfill our duty. I know we will make a good match. So yes."

He touched her arm. Her skin was cold. The warmth of his touch called to her. She moved closer to him as he wrapped his arms around her, pulling her against him. Being a Werewolf, he ran warm. His Wolf stirred in him as they touched.

"Lately, I feel like you have been shutting me out."

Axel wouldn't deny he had pulled back some. *It's better this way. To know would put her in danger.* "Things with the Crazed and the war are changing quickly. I still do not have answers to how they got past our security at our party, or who the traitor is. I can't knowingly put you in harm's way."

"Axel, I'm not some weak, helpless girl. I'm a warrior. Whether you like it or not, the war will involve me too. As keeper of The Realm, it will be my duty to protect it. Keeping me on the sidelines does nothing for either of us."

"As my future and soon-to-be mate, it's my job to protect you."

Leaning into him a bit more, she realized she'd never looked at it that way. "If you want to protect me, you need to trust me and include me. I know you are trying to stop the war, but what will be, will be."

If Axel had anything to do with it, he would try to stop it at all costs. "The timing of our mating is less than ideal with the war on the horizon."

"I don't know if there will ever be a good time. Have you even thought about what you want? I mean outside of trying to stop Erik the Red and the war. Once we are mated then what?" Isla felt the need to ask him, "Do you want a family?" She needed to know where he stood on the topic. A topic that was about to become his reality.

A family? Seriously? "I don't even know why anyone would want to bring a kid into the world at a time like this. To grow up in a time of death and destruction. And children are a distraction. Right now, we need to stay focused on our duty." *The pack comes first.*

Axel's response made Isla's stomach churn. In some ways, Axel was right. They were a great match for wanting to fulfill their duty. She had no choice but to think about their future. Eventually, she would have to tell him about her being pregnant. Would she have to tell him who she was, though? Could she bond with him before he found out? She wished her mom was still alive to give her advice.

CHAPTER 27

Tired of talking, Axel kissed her neck, sending goosebumps racing across her skin. He picked her up in his arms as he took her to his room. Isla let herself relax in his hold, warming herself against his skin.

She was still lost in her thoughts, mulling over what to do next. Isla was ready to get off the rollercoaster she was on. She just wanted things to be normal for a moment. She wanted to enjoy the thought of being pregnant. Enjoy planning her mating ceremony and the union of her pack with Shadow Pack. It was nice to want.

Axel laid her on his bed. He hovered over her as he kissed her. Isla let all of her worries melt away as Axel deepened his kiss. His hands cupped her face before moving down her sides. He broke away from their kiss as he snaked his hands underneath her shirt, lifting it up and over her head, and threw her shirt off to the side. She smelled so good to him. He leaned down and kissed her abdomen as his hands worked to remove her bra, exposing her breast. Massaging them, Axel sucked on her nipples until they hardened. A soft moan escaped her lips. He smiled in response.

She could feel her sex getting wet. Axel smiled as the scent of her arousal filled the room. He pulled her pants off in one quick motion. His fingers trailed up her legs to her inner thighs. Her skin was so soft. Massaging her inner thighs, he pushed her legs open, exposing her sex.

"Let's see if you taste as good as you smell, my little princess." Axel brought his mouth to her sex using his tongue to massage her. Isla lifted her hips in response, feeling the pleasure building in her core. Axel inserted two fingers into her. She was tight and wet.

A whimper escaped her lips, sending Axel into a frenzy. He picked up the speed, teasing her core with his tongue and his fingers. He could feel her tightening as the pressure built up until she lost control as she climaxed.

"That's my princess." Axel settled his hard cock between her legs only pushing the head in and out of her sex.

Isla gripped the sheets. She needed him in her. "Axel…" Hearing his name on her lips brought him to kiss her before she could say anything else. He deepened his kiss as he thrust into her core. She lifted her hips, opening herself to meet his thrusts. Axel's eyes turned black for a moment as his beast clawed, wanting to come out to enjoy the pleasure. Axel fought to stay in control, as he felt her tighten around his sex.

Her hands gripped his back. She dug her nails into him trying to hold on as he thrust harder and faster. Feeling her nails dig into him and her body shutter as she reached her second climax pushed him over the edge, and his seed flooded inside of her.

Axel laid on top of her, carefully not to crush her as they caught their breath. Exhausted, Isla tried to keep her eyes. Axel kissed her and ran his hands through her hair as she fell asleep. Then, he wrapped her in a blanket and carried her to her room, tucking her in before going back to his own bed.

CHAPTER 28

Now that Axel was benched from the field, he was around a lot more. He and Trey had made it their mission to flush out the traitor in their pack before the fastly approaching Gathering.

The first step on his mission was to visit the control room, the hub of the pack's security. Axel paced back and forth waiting on Oliver to pull up all the videos from the night of the announcement ceremony.

Isla monitored the screens closely, looking at which areas of the ground were covered. As much as she wanted to help Axel, staring at the various video camera feeds, she wondered if she could also somehow get Axel to see Duke's one-on-one training session. If he could just see what had happened there would be no doubt that he would change his view on Duke. But she needed to find the right cameras.

Searching the monitor feed Isla found two camera feeds offline. "Which cameras are these?"

Oliver swung over to the screens. "Oh, those are the feeds in the training facility. They've been out for a few days."

Of course they were. "Exactly when did they go out?"

Axel cut in on her little quest. "Isla, they wouldn't provide us with any intel on the night of the gathering. There is no direct line to the ballroom and no exit to the outdoors." He turned his attention back to Oliver. "Who was working security here the night of the ceremony?"

Pushing his glasses back up on his nose, Oliver looked up at Axel. "I was. Lots of action that night."

Losing his patience over waiting for all of the feed that he requested over an hour ago to be cued up, Axel swung Oliver's chair around and pushed it back against the workstation. "I find it interesting that a whole slew of Crazed enters my home to attack my family, and yet a highly skilled pack member like yourself didn't notice a damn thing all night until they attacked."

Oliver sank down as far as he could trying to put a little space between himself and Axel. "I...I..." *I did what I was told to do. I followed orders to watch my assigned area.*

Axel continued to breathe down Oliver's neck pushing him for an answer. Trey stood aside letting his boss take the lead. Isla placed her hand on his shoulder, "Axel stop." Her touch calmed him and he took a breath.

A wave of nausea hit Isla with a force as she became light-headed. Not now. Taking a step back, Isla grabbed the side of the workstation. *Hold it together for a few more minutes. I've got this. I'm ok. I've got this.*

Taking a slow, deep breath, Isla got her footing, and the nausea faded. Axel froze as he was keeping an eye on her in his peripheral vision. He noticed something was off with her. As much as she tried to downplay her brief stumble, he did not miss a beat. His Wolf stirred in worry. Axel backed away from Oliver as Isla took a step forward.

"You said you were the one working the night of the gathering. You're right, there was a lot going on before, during, and after the ceremony's reception. With such a big event and all of these cameras to monitor, who else was working with you that night?"

In her gut, she knew Duke was responsible for this. She just needed Axel and Trey to draw the same conclusion.

"It was just me." *I asked for help. But I don't want to throw my boss under the bus. I did what he told me to do.*

Isla played coy. "With all of these screens how could you possibly manage to monitor all of the security with so many people? What was your job assignment that night?"

Oliver could not spit out the information fast enough. He told them he had direct orders to watch the ballroom hall and the entrance at all costs as his sole priority. With so many visitors entering through the main doors he could barely keep up with who was arriving with who, the security checkpoint at the main door, and what was happening inside the ballroom. The more the ballroom had filled the more he had to watch.

Trey nudged Axel. "She's good."

Axel liked Oliver, so he was relieved he wasn't the traitor. Taking his head off would have been less than pleasing and very messy.

"After our debrief with Garrett I went back through the video footage multiple times trying to figure out what was missed." Oliver started typing away on his keyboard feverishly as screens started to pop up.

The three of them leaned in over Oliver trying to look at the screens.

"I don't follow." Axel wasn't sure what Oliver wanted them to look at.

Oliver rolled his eyes. After selecting the hallway security footage and back door he pointed out the time intervals. "It's so obvious! Watch the bottom of the screen and the shadows, before you and Miss Isla were on the patio, and then after."

Trey spoke up first. "It looks the same."

Oliver lit up with excitement. "Exactly!" He looked at their puzzled faces. Oliver's excitement faded. "Look at the same security footage, same time stamp the day before." Showing the side--by--side comparison, everything started to register.

"The security footage is doctored." The security footage the night of the ceremony had the same footage playing before and after they had been on the patio. This was not good.

As the three Weres started spouting off different theories about who could have doctored the footage, Isla stepped back against the far wall. She could feel a headache coming on. Slowly she turned to walk out of the security room to leave the trio to their debate, trying to go unnoticed.

Before she could exit, however, the conversation halted behind her. She felt Axel come up behind her. "Everything ok?"

As he placed a gentle hand on her shoulder, Isla slowly moved to the side and painted a gentle smile on her face. "Everything's good. I forgot to eat this morning. I have a slight headache, that's all."

He scanned her face looking for a sign she was lying. His look-over ended when Duke walked into the security room. It had been hard enough for Isla to try to keep her nausea in control until she got out of the room, but it became unbearable when he walked in. Her stomach churned violently. Silently she pleaded with the Goddess to let her get out of the room.

"Looks like we have a party in here. Oliver, I don't remember being alerted that you had visitors in the security room, or giving you the authorization to do so."

Duke glanced at Isla before looking at Oliver, who was at a loss for words. Axel had no problem speaking for him. "I didn't know I needed to get your permission to be in my own security room."

As he was addressing the future pack leader, Duke had to choose his words carefully. But "future" did not mean current pack leader. "Of course, but in order for me to do my job it's important procedures stay intact or I can't ensure safety or security."

Oliver cleared the second set of screens of footage before Duke had the chance to look at what they were viewing. "So how can we help you?"

Axel turned to face Oliver and noted the change on the screens. "Oliver already tried. A dead end. I'm surprised you and your team haven't found how the Crazed entered into the ballroom and past the security checkpoints at the entrance."

Duke looked up to see old security footage on the screen. "Yes, we have not had any progress. But please stay if you think you can do a better job or if you think we missed something."

He had never liked him, but now for the first time, Axel did not trust Duke. The smugness in his tone and his arrogance were not appealing to him. When he became Alpha, he would find himself a new second in command. "I find it interesting that with such a large event there was only one person in here to monitor the security cameras."

Duke repositioned himself to stand up to Axel. "The pack leader felt it was a good strategy to have all resources on the ground floor. There was no extra security to spare." *If this bitch is trying to wage war against me, she has a war coming. I was here before her, and I sure as shit will be here after.*

Axel watched Duke's every move, every muscle, every breath he took. His beast was on alert and ready to attack. It was itching to get out if he made one wrong move. Axel wasn't sure why he was so quick to react, it wasn't like him. He was doing everything he could to stay in control. "With the upcoming gathering, I was looking at how we could improve upon our *strategy* for security to ensure everyone's safety. I already had my announcement ceremony infiltrated; I don't want to repeat the same mistakes."

Duke's nostrils flared at the thought Axel could do his job better than him. He was number two and Axel was nothing of rank. For now.

"I've asked Trey to take lead on the security for the next gathering. I told him you and your team would be at his disposal. That way you do not have to stretch yourself too thin between the pack's security and the security of The Gathering. A team approach, working together, has always been Garrett's way of maintaining a strong pack."

Duke nodded though he clearly didn't buy anything Axel was selling.

As Axel and Isla walked out, Trey was left with picking up the pieces of the impromptu appointment. They walked in silence until they were alone.

"*Your* idea? A *team* approach, huh?" Her mocking brought a smile to Axel's face.

"Come on and let's get you something to eat."

CHAPTER 29

Preparations for The Gathering were in full swing. Axel and Trey ran through security details and checkpoints. Meanwhile, they secretly coordinated with The Legion to have them monitor The Gathering remotely though at a close distance, without being discovered.

Isla ran errands with Selene. Selene was a lifesaver in helping her with the finer details of the party. Today's preparations would be the final adjustments before The Gathering tomorrow. There was still a lot to run through. Catering, drinks, arrangements, and décor were all important details packs attending would take notice of. If it was up to her, she would skip all of the formalities. Who cared if packs came or did not come, whether they approved or did not approve. But not showing up to a gathering of this magnitude would be disrespectful, to say the least. Possibly indicating they were no longer allies.

Standing in the fitting room, Isla tried on her dress. When she came out, Selene took a step back because of how stunning Isla looked. Her long, light, silvery blue dress shined under the fluorescent lights. Crystals and beading sparkled like tiny stars in the night's sky. Isla was glowing. "Girl, if Axel hasn't fallen for you already, you will bring him to his knees tomorrow," she said. The thigh-high slit delicately fell open around her right leg as Isla took a step towards the triple floor-to-ceiling mirrors. "You look like a goddess!" Smiling, Isla nodded in agreement: she did feel like a goddess.

After popping a bottle of champagne, Selene handed her a glass of bubbly. The smell of the champagne turned her stomach. "No thank you. Alcohol dulls the senses. I can't afford to be off my game today."

Selene shrugged her shoulders and drank for the both of them. "Well, what do you think?"

Looking at the seamstress she said, "It feels a little tight." The seamstress looked over the dress and put pins where she could let out the dress just a little. Isla took off the dress for the alteration and walked back out to the viewing room in her black silk robe.

"I say you wear the dress as is. It's tight, but you look dead sexy in it. Let Axel rip it off of you at the end of the night," Selene smirked, continuing to drink the champagne.

Isla forced a smile to agree with her. The thought of Axel tearing off her dress was enticing, but the thought of having to wear the tight dress all night brought on a wave of nausea as she broke out in a sweat. "Isla what is going on with you? Are you not happy? Are you sick?"

Slowly, Isla shook her head. "No. I'm just exhausted, worried, and on edge about tomorrow. I just want to get it over with." The smell of champagne filled her nose again. This time she could not keep the nausea down. She made it to the trash can just in time. At least she didn't lose it on the dress. That would have been a disaster.

Selene sat her glass down, rushed over to her, and pulled her hair back. "Are you ok?"

Putting her hand up she assured her, "I'm fine. Sorry. I think I have not been sleeping or eating well." She could feel Selene's suspicion. "I am so worried about tomorrow, I think I'm making myself sick. What if the other pack leaders don't approve of me? What then?"

Selene brought a bottle of water over to her and sat down. "Is that what has you so worried?"

Isla nodded, "That and the possibility of another attack from the Crazed." She didn't dare let her pregnancy slip, not yet. Isla sat down next to the trash can and leaned against the wall. Slowly the nausea started to fade.

Selene understood Isla's worry. Trey had talked non-stop about all of the precautions and possible weaknesses. "Listen, Trey is leading this assignment with no details left out. You could not have anyone better watching your back." Isla agreed. "Plus, Axel will not let anything happen to you. I can tell you two are a great match. He cares for you deeply."

But is it enough for him to have bonded to her? She knew she needed to tell him the truth, all of it, and get it over with.

When the seamstress returned, Isla tried on the dress for one last fitting. Looking at herself, she didn't know if she deserved to put this dress on. Did she deserve to make this fantastic impression at The Gathering tomorrow, knowing she was carrying so many secrets?

The seamstress looked up at Isla in the mirror and nodded in approval. Another work of mastery. She did not say a word about needing to let her dress out. She gave Isla a little extra space and whispered, "It's loose today, but tomorrow it should fit just fine." The seamstress knew. It wasn't her first fitting for an expecting Otherworlder like Isla. Blushing, Isla gave her a nod of appreciation.

She didn't have much to talk about at dinner. Dinner was full of family and friends wining and dining. Isla nodded and acted casual, chiming in on occasion with different conversations. All she could think about was how to tell Axel, to get the truth out. Should she tell him everything at once and get it over with?

She barely touched her food. When everyone started to retreat for the night, Axel gently grabbed Isla's arm for her to stay. When they were alone, he turned to face her. "You hardly ate anything or said a word to me all night. What is going on? And I want the truth." He was worried about her. She wasn't acting herself. His Wolf was worried every time they were near her.

Isla slowly brought herself to look at him in his eyes. They were intense and filled with worry and sorrow. "I'm sorry. I didn't mean to make you feel upset."

His dark brown eyes squinted at her as he watched her very

closely, measuring her response. "If you are having second thoughts about being mated you need to tell me right now." Something was wrong and he could feel it.

His demand caught her off guard. He was so off-base she almost laughed. Almost but not quite. Taking a slow deep, breath, she decided to be honest and truthful with him. No matter the consequence. "No. It's not that. It's not that at all. I just..."

Selene and Trey's timing coming back into the dining hall could not have been worse. "Oh, please Isla, tell me you're still not worried over tomorrow." Selene's voice sounded loud and a little drunk.

Isla needed to just get this over with. "It's just that..."

Selene cut her off as she bounced right into the middle of their conversation. "Axel, she has been so sick and worried over tomorrow."

Selene lightened Axel's mood. He looked at her and smiled. He didn't take her for someone that would worry about things. She was more of an in-the-moment type of person. "Our gathering couldn't be in better hands. Trey has thought through all of the details."

Selene could not have agreed more. "I told her that earlier today." Looking up at Trey she gave him a quick kiss. He was doing good work.

"That's why I wanted to talk to you. To run through a few changes and details."

Axel leaned over and gave Isla a kiss on the top of the head. Any doubt he had earlier melted away, though his Wolf still wasn't at ease.

She would find time soon to tell him. The secrets were going to cost her.

CHAPTER 30

On the day of The Gathering Isla ran around non–stop from the moment she woke up. Axel and Trey had already left to go to the event site to work through the last-minute details. Isla and Selene eventually found their way over to the event space as well, to put the finishing touches on the décor. She saw Axel in passing as he was moving around all business-like and serious.

Walking through the large banquet hall, Isla went through each detail one last time, to see if anything had gone out of place since the last five times she'd checked the decorations. She couldn't care less what people thought. She was looking for any clue that maybe something was tampered with. But everything was in order. She promised herself she would tell Axel everything tonight.

Music filled the air as Isla finished getting ready for The Gathering. Guests were clearly arriving, as she could hear chatter coming from downstairs. She secured the crystal necklace around her neck so it laid perfectly at the center of her chest. It was beautiful, almost as if it was made to go with the dress. She looked at her perfect reflection in the mirror. She didn't feel as perfect as she looked, though. Isla took a deep breath. She needed to get through tonight's gathering in one piece and talk to Axel, to tell him everything.

A light knock at the door drew her gaze from the mirror. Winston entered, dressed in a black-on-black suit. "Isla, you look stunning."

With a quick nod, she said, "Thank you."

Winston stood in place as he looked her over. Her makeup was soft, not overdone. Her hair laid perfectly, not a strand out of place. The glittering shine of her necklace caught his eye. The crystal sparkled like a diamond. "Your parents would have been so proud of you."

How much she hoped that was true. If he knew everything that had happened since he left if he knew she was pregnant, would he still say that?

"I've been told you have been a good guest in the Griffiths' home. You and Axel have been finding time to spend with each other, I take it."

"We have." She was tempted to read his thoughts but decided against it. Winston's opinions wouldn't make a difference at this point anyway.

"Tonight is an important night."

"It is." It was important she told Axel the truth and see where that left them, if she even had a future with him. *I don't even know why anyone would want to bring a kid into the world at a time like this.* Would he view Isla as a distraction? Would he still want her when he clearly did not want children?

Winston studied her with a slight frown. "Isla, is something bothering you?"

Snapping out of her thoughts, she started, "I..." No good would come from sharing her news with her Alpha. She knew if Axel rejected her, she could not return home. Forcing a smile, she changed course. "I think it's time to go downstairs." Winston nodded and opened the door for her.

As Isla left her room she was greeted by Selene, who yelled, "About time!" She escorted Isla down to The Gathering introducing her to everyone she knew—which was almost everyone. Isla nodded and made small talk, but she could not help to occasionally glance around to take note of where security and the wait staff were placed. She noticed that, interestingly, Axel had brought in his personal staff from the club. She was sure that Duke hated giving Axel control over the security decisions and making changes without having any say. The thought brought a smile to her face.

Champagne flutes were passed out by white-gloved waiters with polished gold trays. Isla held her drink in her hand, waiting for the opportunity to discard it. Then, Axel finally made his way across the room to her. He had been watching her from afar since the moment she entered the room. But every time he started to make his way towards her, someone stopped him, wanting to catch up or talk about their continued alliance with the Shadow Pack.

When he finally made it through the sea of guests, he was enthralled. Leaning towards her ear he said, "You look stunning. Just relax and have a good time." Smiling, he gave her a kiss and joined the conversation with the group Selene was introducing her to. Isla looked drop-dead beautiful in her dress, and he was looking forward to taking it off of her later.

There were so many packs and Alphas to remember. How Selene or Axel could remember everyone was beyond her.

Drinks flowed freely and the vibe in the room continued to climb. Everyone was dancing and talking. A perfect picture of unity among the packs.

The music was cut off as Garrett took over the mic. He needed no introduction. His presence on the stage alone brought everyone's attention to him. "It has been ages since we have had a gathering of this size, with such meaning too." Axel pulled Isla in close to him as he wrapped his arm around her waist. She could smell the alcohol on his breath. He had definitely had a few drinks already. She eased into him and relaxed as they looked up at Garrett. Feeling her against his body turned him on, and left him wanting her more, but he needed to pace himself. Duty called. But part of him wanted his duty to be inside of her before the end of the night.

"A little too long if you ask me." The Alphas in the crowd grunted as they agreed. "I could not think of a better opportunity to bring everyone together than to celebrate the union of two Weres who will be mated by the next wolf's moon. Axel has proven himself to be a loyal son and a strong leader. I could not have dreamed of a better son or leader to take my place when I am ready to hand over the reins. Finding a mate strong enough to be his equal was no easy task, but I think I did a pretty good job." The room buzzed with agreement. "Raise your glasses to the future of the Shadow Pack and Midnight Pack coming together to represent peace, life, and overall wellbeing for all of our kind, for many generations to come." Everyone in the room raised their glass and toasted. Isla placed her lip to the glass but did not drink. Just the smell of the champagne started to make her nauseous. She silently prayed to the Goddess that the nausea would go away.

She reached up to Axel to give him a kiss and said, "Excuse me for a few minutes." She retreated to the restroom. She needed a break. The music and the chattering were making her head hurt. Isla gripped the counter as she looked at her reflection in the mirror. All night she had been looking for a sign, something to show history was going to repeat itself. But everything had been going off without a hitch. Everyone loved Isla. A wave of nausea crept up as she tried to calm herself. The blue crystal sparkled brightly in the light.

She needed to get through The Gathering so she could talk to Axel. Desperate to not get sick, she took the crystal off of her neck and loosened the top. Isla sprinkled some of the healing powder into her drink, mixing it. Not the ideal drink, but a sip would not do her harm. Maybe the healing power could ease her morning sickness.

Securing the necklace back around her neck she looked at herself one last time before she rejoined the party. As Isla walked back into the great room, she felt as if something was off. Everyone was on such a high, it was unsettling. Isla stood still in the middle of the room as everyone around her carried on in the oddest fashion. They were laughing about nothing and swaying from one step to the next, lost in the music. Drinks continued to be refilled before they were empty and people continued to drink more and more. She made her way through the mass of guests in their dreamy state, back to Axel.

Axel smiled when she returned. The smell of his alcohol had a weird odor to it. "You're back. Here's a toast to my soon-to-be beautiful mate." Axel, Selene, and Trey raised their glasses, then stopped when they noticed their glasses were empty. "Wait, let's get another round."

The drinks. "There is no need. We can share mine." Before any of them could find a waiter, Isla split her drink among the three empty glasses. "Cheers!"

It wasn't much, but she hoped each glass contained enough of the powder to cure whatever was in their drinks. "I'll go get us some more drinks." She had to get more of the powder in them. Something was way off. She made her way to the bar and waited for the bartender to come over. She needed to get them water. Bottled water. Except, the bartender never came.

Duke slid in next to her. "You don't look like you are having a good time." *You're awfully sober.*

Forcing a smile, Isla tried to act as bright and bubbly as Selene when she was drinking. "I'm having a great time! Can I get you a drink?"

CHAPTER 31

His dark eyes lowered on her as an evil smile crossed his face. "A drink would be great. I'm not sure where the bartender is, but I know where they keep the good stuff. Come with me." Grabbing her elbow, he started guiding her to the door behind the bar.

Isla tried to pull her arm back and stopped. "No. I'm good. I can wait for the bartender. Axel is waiting on me to get us all drinks."

His smile widened. "I don't think Axel will even notice you are gone or remember you went to get him a drink. He's had a few already. I made sure of it." He leaned down closer to her and took a deep breath. "You, on the contrary, haven't been a good guest: refusing to drink to your own toast..." Duke tightened his grip on her arm and pulled her towards the door with force.

"STOP! Let GO of me!" Trying to pull her arm free was not working. Quickly, Isla reached for her whip. However, Duke caught her hand mid-reach.

"No. No. No, you don't." He took the whip off of her wrist and threw it down on the ground as he forced her into the back room. The door slammed behind them, shutting out the noise. As the door closed with a bang, it shut out any chance she had to try to yell for help.

Duke pinned her up against the wall. His sweat had a hint of rancid odor. Fear ran through her veins as she tried shifting her weight to get her hands free from his grasp. If only she could break away and get to her whip, she could wipe the floor with him. Determined, she tried to free herself from his hold. She looked for any weakness as she fought against him. However, it wasn't easy as he was bigger and stronger than her.

"I like some fight in my women." The sound of his cold, deep, dark voice made her shiver in fear. Between the stench coming off of him and feeling the growing erection pressed against her, she was beginning to panic. She had to get out of here!

Calm down. Think. Think, Isla. Duke leaned in to kiss her and she turned her head away. "NO! Stop!"

The more she struggled against him the more turned on he got. His deep laughter caused the hairs on the back of her neck to stand up. His free hand traced down her neck. Down to her breasts. Isla tried to control her breathing but failed. Panic made her heart race. *Oh, God.* His hand traced the side of her body before settling between her legs. She was unable to hold back her emotions as a tear ran down her face.

Everything Axel had taught her about training without her whip started to replay in her head. But looking around she could see nothing she could use to her advantage. *Axel, where are you?*

Duke started to pull up her dress with his free hand and slid his hand through the slit of her dress. Isla tried to move away from him, but he had her securely pinned against the wall.

"That's right. Make me work for it." He leaned in again to kiss her. This time, she didn't move. She let him get close, inches away from closing his lips on hers. When he was close enough, Isla slammed her head forwards, aiming for his nose. Duke bellowed a curse and loosened his grip. Pain shot through her head but she pushed through it, moving as quickly as she could to get away from him.

She willed her body to move faster, as she made her way to her whip which was lying idle by the door. When she hear Duke move again behind her she dived for her weapon. She stretched out her hand, desperately reaching for it. But then Duke let out a terrifying growl as he grabbed her legs, aggressively pulling her back to him.

Another wave of panic flooded her. She frantically tried to kick him to free herself. Duke easily blocked her kicks as he pulled her across the floor, sliding her to him as he sat on her legs pinning her down. "Come here, princess. You are mine."

AXEL! Goddess hear me! Help me. Tears pooled in her eyes. She fought them away. *Stop!* Things weren't supposed to end this way. She would not let them end this way. She couldn't be weak. She had to be strong. Trying to gain control of her upper body, she threw a punch out at him and felt her fist connect to his jaw. Pain radiated down her hand through her arm. She felt the bones in her hand crack as she landed her punch.

Duke returned the act of aggression by backhanding her, slamming her face into the ground. Her ears rang and the burning pain where his hand had landed across her face stunned her. Her vision was blurred, so though she could see his lips moving, she couldn't make out what he was saying. Slowly her senses came back to her. She could taste the blood that pooled on her lips.

Still laying on the ground, she rolled her head back and blinked to refocus her vision and gain control of her bobbing head. Duke pushed her shoulder against the floor with one hand as his other lifted her dress. *NO!* With all of the energy she had left she threw her weight over far enough that she could bite his hand as hard as she could. He screamed as he pulled back. "You fucking bitch!"

Isla pulled herself up and pushed him back enough to get a leg loose. Then, she kicked him with every ounce of strength to free herself. As she got up, she took a quick, deep breath. Disoriented, her body moved sluggishly. She stumbled on her first step as Duke grabbed her by her hair. He pulled her to his face, "You'll pay for that dearly."

"This whole time it was you who planned this! You who betrayed your own pack. For what?" She needed time to get her body to calm down. Pain was shooting down her leg.

Another laugh came out. "I chose the winning side. Besides, you are my reward for everything."

"To work with the Crazed? Bringing them into your pack leader's home?"

"They were an unexpected surprise, I guess you could call them an added bonus to the plan. Turns out my new formula can control Were abilities *and* Crazed. With this powder I will control all Otherworlders. I will be unstoppable."

"The drinks."

"Yes. So easy when everyone loves to have a good drink. Little did I know my new formula would immobilize them. He will be quite pleased."

He? Before she could think about what he meant, Duke threw her back up against the wall. The impact knocked the wind out of her. She tried to spin out of his grasp using the wall as leverage. As Duke pushed her back against the wall she hit it with her head. He had her pinned. She was trapped with no foreseeable escape. Everything started to blur as he tightened his grasp around her neck.

Then, she heard a growl rip through the air somewhere near, though she couldn't see where it was coming from. Two blurry figures bounced into her field of vision. Isla knew one of them was Axel, she could sense him. Closing her eyes, she felt herself slipping away, unable to breathe.

CHAPTER 32

Trey lunged at Duke to knock him away from Isla. She fell to the ground, unable to hold herself up as she gasped for air before losing consciousness. The first attack took Duke by surprise, but he quickly regained his focus. He was champing at the bit for a good fight. He had never liked Trey and he planned on taking him out along with Axel: a two-for-one bonus he would be greatly rewarded for.

Duke launched himself at Trey, transforming into his hybrid Werewolf form. Skin split and bones cracked as his Werewolf emerged. His claws slashed at Trey as soon as he reached him.

Axel froze for a moment when he saw Isla laying on the ground. The sight of her not moving sent every part of his beast into a state of fury. The scent of her blood made him see red. Duke would pay with his life for hurting her, even if it was the last thing he did. Axel's beast took control, breaking through his skin, and setting its sights on Duke.

When Isla regained consciousness, all she could see at first was blurred figures which moved too fast for her to track what was happening. As she blinked, everything started to come into focus. Everything happened so quickly. Trey flew across the room as Duke slammed Axel into the ground. Then, Duke stood over Axel in victory, ready to deliver a death blow. Her chest twisted in anxiety.

Axel! She didn't know if she was thinking it or yelling it but she had to help him. She forced herself to pick up the whip lying by her side. She limped her way close enough to send the whip soaring through the air and wrapping around Duke's neck. Quickly, Isla pulled Duke off of

Axel.

When he felt the pull of the whip, Duke gave into the force of the pull and jumped at Isla.

An angry growl vibrated through the room as Axel flew up and charged at Duke. Muscles rippled down his body full of strength and power as his beast took over, breaking out of his skin. Claws with razor-sharp nails were ready to slice Duke open limb to limb.

Duke was ready for Axel to attack. Duke was taller, larger than Axel, but Axel was stronger. They slashed at each other, ripping skin open. Axel went in for a strike, only for Duke to grab him by the neck and lift him into the air. Trey came from behind knocking Axel out of his death grip, and pinning Duke in a corner. Axel's next strike slashed a large wound into Duke's chest as he went for a kill shot to his jugular, biting him and ripping out a piece of his throat. Duke grasped his bleeding neck, with a look that showed his realization that the wound was too deep for him to heal. His lifeless body fell to the ground.

Axel howled at the victory. His animalist breathing was predatory. Slowly, he calmed his breathing and turned to look at Isla. Any other person would have been petrified of him. To Isla, he was magnificent. Her legs started to feel like jelly. Isla smiled faintly as she leaned against the wall, sliding down to the floor as her legs gave out. She couldn't stand any longer.

Axel went to her side, his beast anxious to see she was ok. Isla lifted her hand weakly and ran it through his hair. She was not afraid of him. She stared at the beast looking at her, as she continued to gently run her hand through his fur. Axel in his Werewolf state was stunning, as he nuzzled her affectionately. Axel had control over his human and hybrid self, a rare ability for a young Werewolf such as himself. As his pulse slowed, he transformed back into his human state, kneeling next to Isla to assess her wounds. Exhausted, she closed her eyes and said, "You came."

He kissed her gently on the head, quietly deciding he wouldn't leave her side for anything. "Of course! When I didn't see you, I felt something was wrong." He didn't know how he had come out of the fog he was in, but he did. Just in time. "A few more minutes. If I hadn't gotten to you when I did, that bastard…"

She put a finger up to his lips. "Shh. You came." The healing powder had worked. Isla closed her eyes again and silently thanked Rattenru. She didn't want to think of what would have happened had she not had the healing powder. "The drinks. Duke, he put something in the drinks."

Axel looked down at her in puzzlement. She had a lot of explaining to do. But it could wait until he got her home safely. Trey walked up to them, holding his head.

"You took a beating."

Trey rubbed his head in agreement. Duke was an excellent fighter and got them both good, but they would heal. He was more worried about Isla. Axel turned back to her and gently wiped away the blood around her face. It angered him she was wounded. Trey listened to his earpiece, giving them a nod. "Everyone inside is still partying, but I think the drug is wearing off. The Legion swept the grounds and found a trace of Erik the Red, but didn't get a beat on him."

It made sense now who "he" was. "Is there a way we can get out of here without being seen?"

Axel picked Isla up in his arms even though she insisted on trying to walk and followed Trey to the exit. He ignored her ongoing protests. This was no time for her to try to show she was strong. He knew she was. She had fought Duke off long enough for him to take him out. He was not letting her out of his sight. Finally, she resigned herself to her fate, she didn't have the energy to push the issue. Relaxing, she rested her head against his chest, giving in as he carried her to the SUV. Trey radioed for Selene and the four of them drove off.

Selene fired off questions regarding what happened, though no one bothered to respond. It wasn't the time. She wasn't happy to wait for details but a look at Isla convinced her to stay in her seat. Axel held her in his lap on the drive home, listening to her every breath, every beat of her heart. He continued monitoring her as she rested against him.

The thought of the danger she had been in made him wish he could kill Duke all over again. *I should have been there.*

"Stop it." Her voice was barely more than a whisper.

"What?"

"Stop analyzing everything." Isla wished Axel would stop blaming himself. No one knew Duke had drugged the alcohol with his formula until it was too late. And there was no way they could have known that he'd made alliances with Erik the Red. Why had he helped out Axel and his team when they were ambushed by the Crazed? It didn't make sense. If he was batting for the other team, why help out the enemy? What did he have to gain by that?

There was so much to discuss. So much information to still figure out. One thing was for sure, Duke did not act alone. And that meant they had a bigger problem on their hands and this fight was far from over. Axel would see every traitor in his pack meet their death for their betrayal and for putting Isla in harm's way.

"You came. That's all that matters."

Axel bit into his arm, offering her his blood. It would help her heal a lot faster than she could on her own. "I will always be there." Accepting his offer, Isla drank from his opened wound. Axel stroked her hair as she drifted off to a dreamless sleep.

CHAPTER 33

Thanks to Axel's blood, her body was healing at a rapid pace. Her fractured hand healed and the bruises on her face were hardly noticeable under her makeup.

Even though she had healed much over the night, Axel insisted she rests the day after, quarantining her in his room. Though he had a lot to take care of, he checked in on her almost every hour. Some check-ins lasted more than others. She wondered if he kept her locked up in his room to tend to her needs to his. Either way, she wasn't complaining.

Today she was on a mission. As she had a lot of time to think about the night of The Gathering she needed to find out who had helped Duke. It didn't surprise her that Duke was behind drugging everyone at the announcement ceremony and again at The Gathering. But he couldn't have done it alone. In fact, with Duke not taking lead on the security detail for The Gathering, how did he manage to still orchestrate tainting all of the alcohol at such a large scale? He had to have had help from inside the pack.

Sitting in the security room Isla kept running through the same footage over and over again. What was she missing?

Trey had done an outstanding job of placing cameras that were easily noticeable but also ones that were hidden. Almost every vantage point was covered.

The goods had been delivered two days before the event. All of the alcohol had stayed boxed until the morning of. No one had touched any of it. In fact, Duke never went near the alcohol. Axel's team from the club stocked and organized everything. The morning, of The Gathering the bar was set up. Everything was in order.

All of his club staff was on deck, running around and organizing everything. Later, they were tending to guests as they arrived and ordered drinks at the bar, with waitresses running orders from the bar to guests. Overall an excellent service. But still no Duke.

After rewinding the footage she went through it again. She kept watching to see when he entered the room. She saw him checking a security detail with Trey, checking in with the security team, and then staying in plain sight of the cameras. Almost like he wanted to be noticed.

Isla's eyes hurt from watching the video feed. She rubbed her temples, trying to push away the strain she was feeling. "We checked all of the security footage yesterday."

The sound of his voice made her swivel around in her chair to look at him. Axel approached her, then wrapped his arms around her. She smiled, glad to see him. "Did you find anything?"

"No." Disappointment was an understatement. He knew they were missing something but couldn't find it. Whoever was covering their tracks was doing a damn good job. But Axel would find the mistake sooner or later.

Axel was glad to see Isla was feeling much better. His hand caressed her face as he tilted her head up towards him. All of his worries melted away now that he was in the same room with her. She grounded him. He bent down and gently kissed her.

A warmth swept over her body as his lips met hers. Her body responded instantly to his kiss. She returned his kiss with more passion as she stood up and wrapped her arms around his neck.

Oliver cleared his throat as he walked into the security room. Blushing, Isla broke away first and started to head for the door. Axel instinctively grabbed her arm and said, "Where are you going?"

Isla turned around with a soft smile. "For a walk. I need some fresh air, a break from staring at the screens."

Axel wanted her all to himself. The brief reprieve from searching for a needle in the haystack was refreshing, but he wouldn't deny her a simple request. Especially when the request had her not working. What was that saying he needed to adopt? Happy mate, happy fate. "Don't be too long." Axel pulled her to him for one more brief kiss and winked at her. He would make sure she would only end up working in one place, and that was under him.

"I won't."

The forest was the one place where Isla felt grounded. This is where she felt most at peace. She followed a small trail up the hill behind the small lake. An easy and peaceful walk to clear her mind. The wind rustled leaves around her, she hoped Rattenru would visit. She needed to thank him. Had it not been for his gift, things would have played out much differently the other night.

What would have happened had she not been able to give the healing powder to Axel? She thought back to how violently Duke had pulled her into the back room without anyone noticing. Everyone was stuck in a state of utopia, reality expelled from their thoughts. It was bizarre. A pack of Crazed could have attacked everyone and they would not have even known what hit them. Whatever drug Duke had used scared her.

Her thoughts started to wander. If Axel had not gotten to her. Had he not been there... *Stop it.* She couldn't think about the what if.

"Isla! Wait up!" The sound of shoes hitting the walking path quickly caught up to her. Cami was catching her breath as she slowed down. "Hey. I thought you could use some company after what happened and all."

CHAPTER 34

"Olli man, what couldn't wait?" At this moment, all Axel wanted was to get to his hot soon-to-be mate. Keeping her within reach is what he needed, he didn't like the thought of her being too far away from him. His beast was restless and wanted her close. It was hard to drown out the thought of catching up to her on her walk. When he did, he could find a quiet little place to do his own little check-up. He smiled at the thought of spending the rest of the day with her underneath him. He had been itching to get his hands on her. A small throb of desire and need started to build. Pushing it down, Axel decided he was giving Oliver ten minutes— no fuck that—five minutes of his time before he would hunt down his women to claim her every way until Sunday. It had already been too long since they last had sex. Three hours was too long. Shit, he knew he was whipped when he thought that.

Trey and Hunter walked into the security room, all business. How many people had Oliver alerted to his big announcement?

Feverishly, Oliver pounded away on the keyboard. Nothing came up on the screens.

Axel didn't have time for this. All he wanted at the moment was to catch up to Isla. "Look, Olli man, when you get to what you want to show us, call me."

Before Axel could turn and walk away the screens changed. "Got it!"

Looking up at the screen, he sighed. He had seen the security footage from The Gathering almost a dozen times. "Olli, I think it's time you got some rest. We already went through these videos. Multiple times."

Oliver shot him a look that stopped Axel in his tracks. "You saw this video feed multiple times." Clicking away at his keyboard Oliver continued. "Whoever tampered with my video feed from the new security cameras was smooth, but not smooth enough."

A few months ago, Axel had Trey and Oliver run a top-secret security upgrade on his club, by running a special grid. The security room had access to the main grid, but not to the backup grid. That one was always running and the second backup was activated when the main grid was tampered with. "I thought your security idea was brilliant, so I toyed with it with our system for The Gathering."

The three of them leaned in and stared at the screens as a new video feed was recovered. Suddenly, Axel had the wind knocked out of him. "What the fuck." Ice ran through Axel's veins, as he could not believe what he was seeing.

CHAPTER 35

Isla really wanted to walk alone. Being out in nature was like a natural recharge. Any chance of Rattenru coming out was squashed with this unwelcomed company. She didn't like Cami much, though it was thoughtful she was checking in on her.

Cami's non-stop, one-way chatter about The Gathering quickly became annoying. "I just can't believe how everything seemed so perfect. It was almost too perfect, but no one cared. The food, the drinks, the music, it was magical. Looking back on it, I can't believe how everything was mystified into a perfect dream. Even Olli looked like a prince." Olli was a good-looking, sophisticated, computer *Were*...if you were into that type of thing, he'd be the complete package. Most females didn't give him a second glance. He was usually the wizard behind the curtain hardly anyone saw.

The thought made Isla a little sad. He was such a likable, sweet guy. Super smart. It was obvious from the way Cami talked about the guests and visiting pack members, however, that a nice guy was not what she was looking for. Nope. She liked the typical dangerous, unavailable, unattainable type. Isla knew girls like her. Always looking for what they couldn't have. Maybe she would find a good mate and things would change. She just needed to stay away from Axel. Which would be hard since she worked for him.

Isla thought about how thankful she was to have been introduced to Axel. Was it because of luck or the fate of the Moon Goddess that they had happened to build a strong connection and feelings for each other? Thinking about Axel made her happy. Deep down she knew she needed to find the time to tell him everything. Let him decide if he wanted to stay with her or not before the mating. Whatever the outcome, she would live with it. A small flutter made her stomach ache. Shit. She needed to go back and eat. No matter what, she needed to take care of the little being growing inside her.

"It was like we were all bewitched by a genie. Except for you. Thank goodness you didn't drink the champagne." As Cami continued to ramble, something struck Isla as odd. Isla slowed her walk. The hairs on the back of her neck stood up in warning. Then, a quick movement in the treeline made her stop altogether. A shadow with deadly red hair and glowing eyes was looking right back at her. Fear ran through her. They were not alone.

CHAPTER 36

They could not believe what they were seeing on the security feed. "That bitch!" He would have her head on a platter. Watching Cami take a package from none other than Erik the Red, right under their noses, made his blood boil.

They watched as Cami added drops of the liquid to glasses before serving a pre-Gathering toast to all of the wait staff, led by Garrett. After a speech of bullshit, everyone drank. They were already drugged before The Gathering had even started.

"The balls of him to walk into my own house. How the hell did he get in?"

Hunter broke the silence and said what no one else would say. "Garrett. He's a dead man. Treason. Conspiring with the enemy. Responsible for drugging the pack and guests at The Gathering. Endangering the life of our future Luna." Olli stopped the video playback of their Alpha, Axel's father, meeting with Erik the Red.

Olli switched the video to this morning's feed. Erik the Red had been here, in his home. Could *still* be here. Meeting with Cami and Garrett. After the meeting, Cami had walked off with purpose and Garrett was drained dry by Erik the Red. Clearly, a trial for Garrett was no longer necessary.

He was here.

A pain of fear struck Axel through his heart and radiated through his body. Every nerve tingled in alarm. "Where is Isla?" he asked coldly. His vision narrowed as he was seeing red. Slowing his breath and controlling his rage, he looked at Olli. "Find her now!"

"Hunter, call The Legion and update them on Erik the Red. Take care of Garrett's body. Bring it to the infirmary room. Trey, lock down and take a team to sweep the grounds."

Axel was seething with anger. After checking his guns were locked and loaded he re-holstered them. His feet were moving in a dead run. His body was on autopilot, following her scent.

Trey and his team ran back and split up, running parallel to Axel in the woods, changing into their hybrid Were form to pick up speed. Time was not on his side. He had to find her before Erik the Red did.

CHAPTER 37

No one had ever said the champagne was drugged. That knowledge was only shared on a need-to-know basis and above Cami's clearance. She was not in the know.

The shadow moved so quickly that Isla didn't know where it went.

Cami turned and faced her. "Oh, Isla. You're a little late to the game." A blunt hit to the back of her head sent her falling to the ground. Lights out.

Isla didn't know how long she had been out. Pain radiated from the back of her head. Slowly her senses came online and she realized she was being dragged. Her arms were sluggish, but she tried to pull free.

"Oh, no you don't." The feeling of a cold, sharp blade against her neck made her freeze. Slowly, her blurry vision cleared. She hadn't gone far. The edge of the hill was only a few feet away. She could see the lake down below.

Erik the Red stood in front of her with his long red hair and evil red eyes. "We have company coming. Take care of her." He took off as Axel closed in on their location, with his gun drawn and aimed at Cami.

A second blade rested firmly against her abdomen. "Stop right there or she's done with."

Axel slowed his approach and kept his aim. Cami shifted behind Isla using her as a shield. His gun stayed aimed with each move.

"Lower your gun, Axel." Cami continued to shift behind Isla, keeping her blades pressed against her stomach. Any wrong move and it would be an easy execution.

"You know I can't do that, Cami. Put your blades down and I will lower my gun."

She met his request with a dark laugh. "She needs to be dealt with. She doesn't belong here. She doesn't belong with you."

Isla looked at Axel. His face was emotionless and deadly. If she could help him get an opening, he would take his shot. She had to try. "Cami, he's just using you."

"Shut up!"

"He left you here to your death. If you kill me, Axel will kill you."

"I said shut up!" Cami dug her blades into her skin, drawing blood. Isla took a deep breath to suck in the pain and tried to shield her abdomen.

"Cami, you need to let her go. It's your only way out of this."

"Only way out of this? The only way out of this. *She* caused all of this. *She* did. She's deceived you and you don't even know it. She isn't supposed to be with you. I am! She isn't even a full Were. She's a fake. A liar!"

Axel didn't let her ranting and raving distract his focus. One shot is all he would get. He shifted his eyes briefly to Isla. "I know." Then shifted his focus back to Cami. "I know who she is. It doesn't matter to me. But she matters to me. She is *mine*."

Cami paused. "You pick her? After all of her lies and secrets. You pick her? How could you? She's not a true Were. *They won't accept you as their leader, or your child.* It's wrong. This is wrong. She's wrong."

They won't accept you as their leader, or your child. Her words echoed through Axel's head as he tried to register what Cami said. Confused, he looked at Isla. A tear ran down Isla's face.

Cami dropped the blade from her neck. "This is so precious. You didn't know." Evil laughter escaped Cami.

Time slowed. Isla felt the blade piercing into her abdomen, digging deeper. She turned away, trying to free herself from Cami. Screaming in pain, she tried to knock away her hand.

Suddenly, Cami threw Isla towards the edge of the cliff. Isla stumbled, trying to gain control of her body as she was flung with force to the edge of the overhang. Gun fire was the last thing Isla heard as she lost the fight to find her balance, falling over the side of the cliff down to the lake. *The lake will be there for you when you need her.*

"Isla!" Axel sprinted towards her as he watched her disappear over the edge. Without a second thought he went after her, taking a leap of faith off of the cliff. As he dove into the dark water searching for her, fear motivated him to find her. Fear of losing her. Fear of never being able to tell her he loved her. Fear of losing everything.

CHAPTER 38

A dim light in the water guided him toward her direction, lighting a path. He could see Isla suspended in the water, unmoving. He grabbed her, then swam to the surface using all of his strength to pull her to the shore.

Everything around Axel was a blur. From Hunter and his team helping them to shore, to the chill of the night that met him after he surfaced from the water. His warriors quickly took charge and rushed Isla off to the infirmary. He followed them with his last ounce of energy. To hell with anyone who thought he needed to rest or get himself checked out. He was not leaving her side for a moment. The only thing that mattered in this moment was her.

He watched as the doctor and his nurse worked on her. Occasionally, the doctor glanced up to look at Axel, who was staying still as a statue. Watching. Waiting. The beast inside him was afraid. Laying and waiting. There would be hell to pay if she wouldn't make it. If she didn't make it, he wouldn't either.

The silence was deafening. He wanted answers. An update. But no news was good news. He didn't dare say a word or make a noise that would take the medical team's attention away from Isla and the baby. *Our baby.* Closing his eyes he prayed for a miracle. The picture of Cami digging the blade into her abdomen, the tears running down her face, was the only thing he could see. There was no need for words. *I should have shot her sooner. Maybe, just maybe I could have shot her before she stabbed her with the blade.* Thinking back, he realized there had been no safe shot he could have taken without risking shooting Isla. He had a great aim, but he couldn't have risked her life like that.

"That's it." The doctor finished closing up Isla's wound, bandaging it, as the nurses cleared the area. Moving a chair to her bedside he motioned for Axel to sit down.

"What do you mean, that's it?" Axel barely recognized the tone of his own voice. He had no ounce of energy left to contain himself. Emotions were starting to pour out of him.

"Sit." It wasn't a request but a command. As soon as he sat down, he felt all of his energy drain out of him.

"Miss Isla endured a deep wound very close to the fetus. But the bleeding has stopped. She will recover."

A sense of relief eased him a little. Looking at the monitors, the wires, and the beeping, a pain grew in his chest. "What about the baby?"

"We will monitor both of them closely and do everything we possibly can." He would make no promises, no guarantees. Axel was left in silence as he sat at her bedside.

He wasn't sure how long he had been asleep when the door opening woke him. Immediately, he grabbed one of his guns, ready to protect his mate at any cost.

Rattenru entered with two of his personal guards. "At ease, son." Axel re-holstered his weapon without taking his eyes off the creature. The guards stayed by the door but close enough to attack if need be. Rattenru approached Isla, looking over the monitors before scanning her with his hand. He smiled.

"You had a choice to go after Erik the Red but you chose Isla in the end. Had you gone after Erik, you would have caught him and ended him."

"Perhaps."

"Ah, no. I saw it, dear boy. You would have had a glorious battle against Erik the Red. A glorious victory, in fact."

Rattenru didn't need to look up at Axel to read his emotions. He could feel them. There was no regret. He continued moving his hand over Isla's stomach. A glow warmed between them as he hovered over her. As soon as he moved his hand away, he finally looked up at Axel.

Axel broke the brief silence. "I would do it all again. Saving her. She's mine."

Rattenru nodded. "A worthy mate for a worthy princess. You both have my blessing. She will recover. Together you will be great leaders, writing history together."

Before Rattenru reached the door, Axel called after him, "What of our baby?"

Briefly, Rattenru turned back to look at Axel. "He is very strong."

Relief humbled him and he said, "Thank you." He. Axel lit up inside.

"Don't thank me. Thank the Lady of the Lake. She gave the gift of healing. Honor her well." Without another word, the Fairy's leader left with his royal guard.

Axel went back to Isla's side. He gently brought her hand to his mouth and kissed it. He was overcome with gratitude that she would survive. Then, she stirred and tried to sit up, but Axel kept a hand on her shoulder. "Shh. Lay back and rest."

Isla's eyes fluttered open. It was like seeing her for the first time. She was beyond beautiful. She was his. He couldn't stop himself from kissing her forehead.

Isla looked around to assess where she was at. The last thing she remembered was standing on the cliff of the hill and... She touched her stomach where she was bandaged and noticed the wires wrapped around her. "Axel?" Worry brought tears to her eyes.

Smiling, he said, "You both are going to be fine." Looking over at the monitors she saw the rhythms of two heartbeats. A sense of relief washed over her.

"I'm so sorry I didn't tell you." She could not hold back the tears pooling in her eyes.

Hushing her, he kissed her. Comforted her. "All that matters is that you both are okay." Their embrace was interrupted by a knock at the door.

"What is it?" he snapped. He had told them he did not want to be disturbed.

The door opened to reveal Hunter with a grim look on his face. Whatever it was, it wasn't good. And Isla didn't need to be bothered with negativity. Axel leaned over to kiss her. "I'll be right back."

As Axel stood up, Isla gripped his hand, stopping him in his tracks. "Hunter, it's okay, come in." Hunter looked from Axel to Isla, who gave him a reassuring nod. They were in this together. No more separation.

Hunter closed the door behind him, unsure how to proceed with what he had to say.

Taking a deep breath, he decided to just blurt it out. There was no good way to say it. "Sir, Trey..."

Isla gasped, "Oh, no."

"How?" Axel kept hold of Isla's hand. He never thought he would want or need her support upon hearing of the loss of one of his pack members, a close friend. But feeling her grip on his hand was comforting.

Sadness filled him as he listened to Hunter. "Trey went ahead of the pack, going after Erik the Red. He was outmatched. By the time we caught up to him he was already down."

CHAPTER 39

"Are you ready for this?" Isla couldn't help but ask him. He had said very few words all day. Today would be a test. A test of Axel's determination to lead. A test to see if the pack would follow him.

He nodded. He knew what he needed to say. "No matter what, we will do this together."

The chatter that had filled the great room stopped when they walked up front and center. He had rehearsed his speech all day. Hunter and Oliver had proofed his speech, and grilled him on what to say. Axel stood center stage as he faced his pack members and guests. His eyes swept the audience. The Legion and members from other packs were gathered for the first time ever in this very room. History was being made.

The speech he had prepared and rehearsed was a good one. A well-written, political speech that would appeal to the elders in the group. It said exactly what they wanted to hear him say. Glancing back at Isla he extended his hand to her, pulling her to his side. *Together we are stronger.*

He was not going to stand before his people and give them a speech that had been written and rewritten with an eye to what the elders wanted to hear. No. He was going to stand in front of everyone and speak his truth. Everyone in the room had a choice to make and it needed to be their choice.

"*We* stand before you as we face unimaginable circumstances. War is upon us. We can either fight for what is right or wait for it to tear us down one by one. We need to fight for our families and our loved ones." Axel looked at Isla and found more strength than he could ever ask for. The loss of Trey— a warrior, his friend—and the memory of almost losing Isla and their baby gave him clarity on what he needed to say.

Axel looked his pack members in the eyes as he continued, "For our children and children's children, we must unite and stand together. The war came to our doorstep the night the Crazed infiltrated our home and attacked our own. But this war is like no other. There will be lives lost...lives have already been lost. But no life lost will be in vain. What I can promise you, is that I will fight alongside you for all the same reasons why you should be fighting. For our children to grow up in a world where there is no war...to not be caged. To live and be free. But we cannot fight this war alone. We have to work together. We have common enemies: Erik the Red, the Crazed, and those who follow him."

Axel spoke from his heart. He looked at Selene, who was sad but standing tall. Only a few knew the truth about his father's betrayal of the pack. They had told everyone Garrett was killed by Erik the Red and left it at that. It would do more harm than good if people knew he had been a traitor.

Chatter broke out in the back of the room. The elders in front kept their faces guarded, not showing any emotion. Axel thought about his next steps. He wanted to give everyone a choice for their own future. His father had ruled with fear and strength. Axel was going to be a leader people trusted and worked with out of respect. Garrett put power and greed first and it only got him killed in the end. That would not be the path Axel would follow.

He wasn't sure what to do next as the chatter died down. Hunter was the first one to step out of the crowd in front of Axel. "I will follow you." He took a knee and bowed. The majority of his former pack members took a knee around him and similarly pledged their allegiance. Axel noticed a few elders walking to the back of the room to leave. Axel tried to hide his disappointment that they were not willing to change.

When the trickle of warriors who pledged their allegiance halted, Griffin approached Axel. Standing in front of him, he pledged they would be allies as long as they worked together to achieve the same goal. Shaking his hand, he accepted the alliance. Griffin would not take a knee to anyone, but his handshake was good enough for Axel. Griffin looked at Isla and nodded to her.

This was only the start of the war. Axel would go after Erik the Red and avenge those who had lost their lives, ridding this world of Erik's evil. With his son on the way, he had a new purpose to fight. Rubbing her expanding belly, he kissed Isla. "Come with me."

As they walked out to the lake he stopped and looked up at the moon. Silently, he thanked the Moon Goddess for finding him his mate. The crowd that remained followed them, gathering outside. "I owe everything to you and to the Lady of the Lake." He led her into the water until it reached their ankles. "I love you Isla. I could not ask for a better mate to stand by my side. I can never thank the Lady of the Lake enough for saving you both."

Isla was at a loss for words, but her heart swelled with love. Her smile was brighter than the moon itself. Axel kissed her passionately. His need for her grew harder. "You are mine."

"I am yours." She cupped his face, returning his kiss.

Axel playfully bit her lower lip as he trailed kisses down her neck. Instinctively she leaned her head to the side. His canines elongated. It pleased him how easily her body responded to him. Her exposed neck was called to him. Axel bent down to her neck, biting her, marking her. He pulled away and bit into his arm so she could take his blood, completing their blood bond.

The crowd howled in approval as their Alpha claimed his princess. Their Luna. Axel looked up and nodded as their pack returned to the house, leaving them in privacy.

There was one step left to complete their mating ritual. He had her, marked her, and now he would claim her—connecting their souls for eternity.

Isla was in a state of euphoria. His bite had turned her on uncontrollably. She felt herself grow wet with desire. She could not get her clothes off fast enough.

Leading her deeper into the water, he kissed her. She ran her hands over his body, exploring him as his beast took over to claim her. Her beast. Her Werewolf. He was magnificent. Strong. She owned him and he knew it. His beast knew it.

Isla took the lead, bringing his hands to her stomach which was evidence of what grew inside of her. He groaned in approval. Words were not needed for the love they shared. She reached up to him, needing him to be inside of her.

It took everything in him to control the need to claim her hard and fast. He took it slow, letting her mount and ride him. His control only lapsed when she called for him, "Axel!"

He cut his neck, letting her feed from him as they mated. Feeling her suck his neck made his sex kick inside her. She felt the building pressure in her core, coming close to reaching an orgasm.

"Not yet." He growled at her. He wanted to orgasm with her, to mark her with his seed. No male would dare come near her without scenting him on her. A warning she was his. He gripped her hips and lost control. Growling he met her climax and released inside of her as she gave in to her own pleasure. He marked her over and over again. She kept a tight grip on his shaft, pulling him deeper, wanting all of him until he finished.

He held her as she released her grip on him, transitioning out of his hybrid state. Picking her up, he wrapped her in his arms and carried her to his bed. He was not finished with her. No, he was just getting started.

-The End-